W9-COH-155

THE

AMBASSADOR

OF

WHAT

STORIES

ADRIAN MICHAEL KELLY

a misFit book

Copyright © Adrian Michael Kelly, 2018

Published in Canada by ECW Press
665 Gerrard Street East
Toronto, Ontario, Canada M4M 1Y2
416-694-3348 / info@ecwpress.com

All rights reserved. No part of this publication
may be reproduced, stored in a retrieval system,
or transmitted in any form by any process —
electronic, mechanical, photocopying, recording,
or otherwise — without the prior written
permission of the copyright owners and ECW
Press. The scanning, uploading, and distribution
of this book via the Internet or via any other
means without the permission of the publisher
is illegal and punishable by law. Please purchase
only authorized electronic editions, and do not
participate in or encourage electronic piracy
of copyrighted materials. Your support of the
author's rights is appreciated.

This is a work of fiction. Names, characters,
places, and incidents either are the product of
the author's imagination or are used fictitiously,
and any resemblance to actual persons, living or
dead, business establishments, events, or locales
is entirely coincidental.

Get the
eBook free!*
*proof of purchase
required

Purchase the print edition
and receive the eBook free!
For details, go to ecwpress.com/eBook.

LIBRARY AND ARCHIVES CANADA
CATALOGUING IN PUBLICATION

Kelly, Adrian Michael, 1967–, author
The ambassador of what : stories /
Adrian Michael Kelly.

A misFit book.
Issued also in electronic formats.
ISBN 978-1-77041-417-4 (softcover).--
ALSO ISSUED AS: 978-1-77305-253-3 (ePUB),
978-1-77305-254-0 (PDF)

I. TITLE.

PS8621.E44A812 2018   C813'.6
C2018-902549-2   C2018-902550-6

MISFIT

Editor: Michael Holmes/
a misFit book
Cover design: David A. Gee
Author photo © Melissa Howlett

The publication of *The Ambassador of What* has been generously supported by the Canada Council
for the Arts which last year invested $153 million to bring the arts to Canadians throughout
the country, and by the Government of Canada. *Nous remercions le Conseil des arts du Canada de
son soutien. L'an dernier, le Conseil a investi 153 millions de dollars pour mettre de l'art dans la vie des
Canadiennes et des Canadiens de tout le pays. Ce livre est financé en partie par le gouvernement du Canada.*
We also acknowledge the Ontario Arts Council (OAC), an agency of the Government of Ontario,
and the contribution of the Government of Ontario through the Ontario Book Publishing Tax
Credit and the Ontario Media Development Corporation.

Ontario
Ontario Media Development
Corporation

ONTARIO ARTS COUNCIL
CONSEIL DES ARTS DE L'ONTARIO
an Ontario government agency
un organisme du gouvernement de l'Ontario

Canada Council
for the Arts

Conseil des Arts
du Canada

Canadä

PRINTED AND BOUND IN CANADA   PRINTING: WEBCOM   5 4 3 2 1

MIX
Paper from
responsible sources
FSC
www.fsc.org   FSC® C004071

To B. & D.
Forward

We are children for a very long time.

ADAM PHILLIPS

ONE

ONE

STRAGGLERS

———————————————————————————————

My molar, it hammered me. I groped for the clock and turned the yellow-green glow of its hands away. 3:15 a.m. Go and get some Orajel, or put an aspirin on it, but we had no hallways, only rooms. Dad would hear.

I waited.

⌐

We lived behind the Acropolis. Our landlords were the owners, and I could hear them in there now. Elena sang a song in Greek, stacking plates and saucers. Nik fried an onion. He always did that first. The smell of it bustled sharp and strong through the heating vent. I got out of bed. Any normal Saturday, we were already up an hour and slogging down the road.

⌐

Dad was having apnea. I peed loud and flushed, and had a look at my tooth in the mirror. The gum beneath it bulged. I pressed it and I tasted it, the poison of myself. A pair of aspirins in my palm. One I swallowed at the fridge with skim. The other I wedged in the cavity. My mouth knew to make more spit.

⌐

Onion filled the flat now. I opened the door and screen. Rain pocked the river. In for a landing on the embankment came a fat and filthy gull. It waddled underneath the deck, where torn-open bags of Acropolis trash filled the stinking big blue bins. Other gulls were scrumming there. That hideous heads-up gape-beak screaming.

⌐

Dad yawned and did a fart. I went to his door.
    Tea?
    Aye.
    Cream of Wheat?
    Eggs, how bout?
    Hard or soft?
    Soft, mine.

Soldiers too?

He did the English: I say, soldiers *do* sound jolly good.

I said, Indubitably, but when I filled the kettle up, my hand shook, my whole arm.

⌐

More tea? I said.

Time we got that car unloaded.

Raining pretty hard.

Made of sugar?

No.

Right. Let's get it done.

Dad was an odd combination, part-time on the ambulance, full-time painter-decorator. The Bel Air smelt of Varsol. Ladders rode the roof. We took them off and chained them to the railing around the deck. Rain dripped from our noses. Dropsheets big as sails and heavy, gallons and quarts and pints of paint, the machine for stippled ceilings, we unloaded all of that and plunked it on the kitchen floor. I pulled the cling of my T-shirt free.

Shower now? I said.

Aye. Don't dilly-dally.

I stepped around the tools and gear in soaking wet sock feet. Imagine if I fell. All these hard, edged things.

⌐

Pink and clean as new pork cutlets. I put on my Wrangler jeans. The brown plaid Western dress shirt. Tomorrow I hadn't decided. The one was a real Bill Rodgers singlet. It had a blue band across the chest. The famous BR logo. Dad got it me in Boston. The other was from my school. A gift from VP Evans. Heck of a thing you're doing, son. Hope you'll be our ambassador. The shirt was yellow as corn on the cob. Halfway down the front it had a tall green pointy star. Skinny letters in the star said p H s. No one would have a clue what they meant, but I had red shorts with a yellowy stripe, and none with any blue. The longest time I stood there, staring at one and then at the other. Finally went with yellow and green. Ambassador of what.

—

Dead leaves plastered Highway 30. We passed the Klaussen farm. Holstein cows, their udders and their arses caked, plodded up a slant of mucky barnyard. High in the air over Pine Ridge, a hawk tilted in the wind and rain. Dad rolled down his window. The wiper had started to stagger. He reached out, and gave it a flick. Then he sniffed.

Fuck no.

I looked at the gauge. The lean of the needle.

He banged the dash. Filthy *cunt*.

I sank in my jacket.

—

We pulled in at the Shell near Brighton. Dad got out and popped the hood. Squalls of steam escaped. Round to the back of the wagon he went and swung the tailgate open. Cool air rushed inside the car. He unlatched his first aid kit. Took out tape and gauze and swabs, a pad.

You, he said. Off your arse.

I met him round the front.

He said, Get your coat off. Hold it up and keep this dry.

The radiator hose had split. He swabbed it like a dirty wound. Applied the sterile pad. Wrapped gauze around it. Then tape. My arms ached. The back of me, soaked. He lowered the hood.

Wait in the car.

Came back with a brimming bucket. Uncapped the rad, and filled it.

To have talons and wings and far-seeing eyes. To think just perfect hawk thoughts.

In the slow lane on the 401, he kept it under sixty. Truckers passed and shot us looks. The car was trailing scarves of steam. Up the way on the other side, I saw the yellow Fifth Wheel sign, and I pointed to it. Dad whacked the blinker. At the exit, turned left on a red. Ahead of us, a transport crept, belching black exhaust. Dad pulled out and had a look. Passed on a solid line. We rolled to the edge of the Fifth Wheel lot, and the car let go its last. I stared at wet macadam.

Needin a pee?

I shook my head.

Wait here, then. Won't be long.

He walked through a puddle as big as our flat and didn't seem to notice. The camera was in his Adidas bag. When he had gone inside, I pointed it at my face. I hate this, I said, and I don't want to be here, but I didn't press the trigger. I didn't have the guts. Anyway, it had no mic. I would be a silent movie. Have to read my lips.

⌐

We split a Kit Kat. I chewed on the side with less decay and waited for him to talk. He only sat there, quiet as crags.

I said, What's happening?

He said, How do you mean?

We going home?

He looked at me. Kiddin?

I didn't speak.

Denny's on his way, he said.

What about the car?

It'll have to be towed.

Are we getting it back?

He stared out his side.

⌐

Not to tell it now was hard, but I had promised her. After the wedding, when we had a few days, Mum took me to the track. Her fat bald bookie gave us tips, but I bet on my hunches. Seven hundred was my half. We opened my first bank account. The balance was earning interest. I thought he would feel it. I thought he would see. My face was scarlet. Words were storming my throat and mouth, but I quelled them. I was rich.

⌐

He looked at his Seiko.

Fuck's Denny?

The rain had gone for a coffee break. I said, Out and walk?

Aye. Good idea.

We swung our arms and stretched. Feeble sun showed its face. Gulls mobbed the Fifth Wheel bins and fought for scraps in the parking lot. Through diesel fumes and fryer grease came whiffs of Lake Ontario, a cold stew of seaweed and half-rotten fish. Then a horn honked. Denny flashed his lights. I waved high and hard.

Gaw, son, look at the size of ye.

Iain didn't come?

He's in Long Island. Your dad no tell ye?

I shook my head.

Tournament, said Denny. You'll see him Sunday night. C'mon, hop in. Car's warm.

I'll just get my bag.

Leave it, son. I'll get it.

He and Dad shook hands.

Pal.

How are ye?

It made me want a brother. The history in their eyes.

⌐

Eighty miles an hour, and the LeSabre felt like CP Air, cruising altitude. A wall ran along the far right lane, and Denny pointed past it. Mud and model homes.

I'm puttin carpet in half these places.

Dad only nodded.

Clamorin for trades.

No doubt they are.

I know a guy—Ahmed. His son plays wi' Iain. Hell of a foot. Anyway, he's a painter. Remember Joyce McClure?

No.

Blond wee thing. Markham Road.

Peterhead?

That's her. Done all right, Joyce has. A.E. LePage. Her youngest plays wi' Iain too. Along at a game the other day, she says to Ahmed, Come round mine for an estimate, like? He says, You couldn't afford me. She says, Beg your pardon? He says, You couldn't afford me. The face on her. Know what I mean? I says to him after, Ahmed, could you no gie her a break? He says, Denny, I get what I'm worth. Take a guess.

No idea.

Twenty-five.

An hour? I said.

Aye, son. An hour.

Dad squared his shoulders. Thinkin of backin off on the paintin. Go full-time on the ambulance.

That right?

Dunno yet.

Denny looked in the rear-view mirror. How 'bout you?

Me?

Aye. How do you feel?

About what, Uncle Denny?

Movin back here.

I looked at Dad. At his neck, the creases.

Where we are is fine, I said.

Talking stopped 'til Agincourt.

20

The street made a circle round a small park, where an old man watched his bony mutt squeeze out spindly turds. We pulled in the drive. Aunty Ag was watching us out the picture window, arms crossed under her big cone breasts.

Come let me see ye.

I pecked her cheek.

Skinny malinky. She looked at Dad. No feed'n this wan?

Your accent's fadin.

She made a fist. Shut that door. Ma heat's fly'n oot.

Heat on for?

Baltic the day. Shoes! Anywan marks ma carpet, I'll brain him.

Bet you've missed this. Denny winked.

Have yez had a bit tae eat?

Could do with a bowl of soup, said Dad.

Right. Denny'll take yez doon the stair.

Into the perfect house we went. Even the basement smelled of Glade.

I was allowed an Irn-Bru. The soup was beef and barley. Warm rolls as well. Came a lull in the blether, and Aunty Ag said, Do ye hear from your sister?

I looked at Dad.

He was out to Calgary a month ago.

Thanks. I was ask'n him.

Dad gave a nod.

For the wedding, I said.

Aunty Ag stopped chewing. Whose?

Janice.

You're jok'n.

No.

Age is she now?

Twenty-one?

God in Heaven. She looked at Dad. Why have you no telt us?

He shrugged. Forgot.

Who's the fella?

Tim, I said.

Tim what?

Troffer.

What does he do?

Plays hockey.

Professional?

Semi. In Spokane.

Where's tha?

Washington State, said Uncle Denny. Janice movin there?

I don't know. Guess so.

It got quiet, but Aunty Ag said it.

Was your mum at the wedd'n?

Yes, I said. My chest was tight. Janice's dad as well.

Together ye mean?

Agnes, said Denny.

I'm only ask'n.

No, I said. He has a new wife.

How is your mum?

Spoilt him, said Dad.

Aye, first time she's seen him in—

Agnes, said Denny. Leave it.

We ate. Current hummed in the clock on the wall.

⌐

In the unfinished part of the basement, I turned on the bare light bulb and knelt in front of the cubby-hole. Evel Knievel, G.I. Joe, Big Jim, Batman, Stretch Armstrong, and Star Wars characters (even the cantina creatures) were jumbled together in two milk crates. I slid them out, and scooched in for a look at the stack of games. Simon was on top. The batteries worked. Cross-legged on the cool grey floor, I began to play. Four coloured tabs, red, yellow, blue, and green, each with its own sound, lit up in random sequence. You had to repeat the sequence by pressing on the tabs. It started slow and easy, say, red, blue, blue, green, but the more you got right, the faster and longer the sequences got, red-red-blue-green-blue-yellow-red, on and on, more and more. There is a kind of trick to it. Don't stare at the tabs. Let your eyes go soft. Let your hand remember. Only on Level 4 could the computer begin to beat me.

⌐

Dad thumped down the stairs. Fuck's that?

Game.

Get it off.

Sorry.

Togs, he said, and nodded at the finished room.

We're going for a run?

Bit a film is all.

I thought today was resting.

Half a wee lap a the street.

In we went and changed. Wearing my shorts and shirt felt wrong, like premature delivery. I thought they might be angry and take revenge tomorrow, siphon off my strength. In my head I told them sorry. Asked them for permission and promised we wouldn't be long. I wouldn't sweat or get them dirty. Right back in the bag they'd go. Resting. 'Til tomorrow.

Denny blew on his hands. Sure ye want to do this now?

Dad shrugged. Sun's out.

Give us the camera, then.

I'll get the lad on his own first.

Fine. I'll scratch my arse.

Dad ignored him and looked at me. Top of the street. Run back.

I cut through the park at a medium jog. Rust speckled the swing set. A Becker's bag blew by and caught in a wobbling bush. Then I stepped in a squish of shit. Scraped my shoe on the curb and retched. Dad was waving, *Go.* I gave the legs a little gas, but before I entered the final bend, he had taken the camera away from his face, and I saw the disgusted slits of his eyes.

Back, and do it again.

Wrong wi' it? said Denny.

Again, said Dad. Put some umph in it.

Have ye asked him if he wants to?

The face on Dad.

Denny looked at me. Eh, son? Do ye want to do this now?

I nodded.

Just say—

Uncle Denny. It's all right.

This time I got set, and took off like track. A 1500-metre pace. Into the bend I went even harder.

Okay, kid. Got it.

I pretended not to hear him.

Ease up, he said. EASE UP.

Those half seconds. When both my feet are off the ground. When I'm full-out, and the air is streaming.

⌐

Downstairs in the finished room, he pointed to the floor.

Here.

I stood where he said, and saw it coming. BANG, above the ear.

What in fuck was that?

You said put some umph in it.

Could have pulled a muscle.

We don't even have a projector.

BANG, opposite side.

It's true.

BANG, back on the left. Anything else to tell me?

No.

Eh?

Sorry.

Go and give your face a wash. Comb that hair as well.

Off he went upstairs. In the basement washroom, I ran

the taps awhile and put an aspirin in my molar. It was a lie what he told Uncle Denny. Full-time needed EMCA. He had passed the practical, but completely bombed the written. Could barely even spell.

⌁

Big spaghetti nosh-up. My belly out to here. I helped Aunty Ag with the dishes, then she and Denny went to get dressed. They were off to a ceilidh come eight o'clock. *ShaNaNa* would be on telly now, but Dad told me to come downstairs.

Here, he said. Get this in you.

It looked like a square of Jersey Milk. I asked him what it was.

Laxative, he said.

I'm not bunged up.

Flushes you out. Won't have to stop tomorrow.

We just carbo-loaded.

So?

Will I not poo them out?

Don't be daft. Mild, that. Works overnight.

You taking one?

Course I am.

I did the English. *Down* the hatch.

⌁

In the living room. Full regalia, Denny. The shine of him, the swish. His sporran had a face. I asked him it.

He said, Stoat, and fiddled with his Pentax. Handed it to Dad. Wait 'til the flash—

26

I can manage.

In came Aunty Ag. A matching kilt and sash.

I said, You look smashing.

She curtsied, Thank you, son, and put her arm round Denny. Oor first night oot in ages, pal.

Dad said, Ready? and counted three. My aunt and uncle smiled. It wasn't fake, it was married. Away they went trailing aftershave and perfume. Dad put the telly on. I had never seen *CHiPs* in colour.

⌐

To tread on the carpet would have been sin. It still had the Hoover marks. No damp towels, twists of ginch. No wrinkles and no dust. Posters of Styx and Kevin Keegan and a Glasgow Celtic scarf and strip were pinned to the walls but perfect, like geometry. On the desk, a globe. *Encyclopedia Britannica*. Not once had I ever been in this room, even when Iain was here. *Wish Book* room. Perfect room. I turned off the light. On the ceiling, planets and stars glowed green-yellow. I closed the door and went downstairs, where Dad was gargling Listermint. He didn't brush at all anymore. It only made him bleed.

⌐

Falling asleep, he twitched and flailed, swore in slashing whispers. I lay rigid on my back, thinking he would wallop me, maybe even strangle me. At last came his snore. I nodded off, but woke with a clench and ache in my guts. Slow as a hostage, I eased out of bed, and on the way to the toilet, let

slip a fart. The shock of it. The burst. I bolted the rest of the way, and barely got sat down. Soft shit blasted out of me. Then a spray of muddy flecks. Dollops of Grey Poupon in my ginch. I stared at them aghast. Didn't flush. Stuck my head out and listened. He hadn't wakened. A bag lined the wastebin. Maybe ten minutes I took on the stairs. Every creak an agony. Gently out the side door. Feet cold against flagstone. Wind on my bare and burbling arse. I threw the bag like plastic parachute army men. It landed plop on the roof next door.

I made a bed of the bathroom mats. Aunty Ag had great towels, very soft and thick. One I folded and made my pillow. The other was my blanket. Every ten minutes for the first while, I was up and on the crapper, farting out my dregs. Then it got better. I thought stoats should be stoats, not sporrans, and finally, I slept.

My body was its own alarm. I heard him yawn and stretch.
Son?
Shot up and turned on the light. Flushed away the thick shit pudding.
Can I get in?
Minute please.
I sorted the mats and one of the towels and wrapped the other around my waist. Gave my face a splash.
Come on, boy. I'm bustin.

Gaped my eyes as wide as I could and pasted on a grin.

Morning!

Shh. Not so loud.

Sorry.

I ducked by. In he went for his number two. I put on my shorts and lay on the floor, one leg extended, the other pulled toward my chest. Dad shaved. To clean his razor of bristles and cream, he slooshed it in the steaming sink and then tapped it on the edge. Usually three. Tap-tap-tap. Today it wasn't like that. Today it was idiot Morse. Denny lent him styptic.

We lined up well back in the field and pinned our numbers on. Dad was 1454. I was 1456. A short man right in front of me had curly hair like McEnroe, and the back of his light blue T-shirt said, *Warning: I spit left*. The Labatt logo was everywhere. A cop on a horse, its rippling rump. Denny had taken our photograph beside the statue of Edward VII, but I forgot until I saw it later. The stink of portable toilets. I remember that. Anything solid, I would have sicked up, but breakfast had been electrolytes, dissolved in a glass of water.

Calm now, lad. Big deep breaths.

Vicious wind, I said.

Find someone. Tuck in behind.

Up ahead, the gun went off. A lot of the other runners cheered. We inched along. Then a slow jog.

Remember what I've telt you. Nine minute miles.

Nine minute miles.

Fluids.

Every station
Two cups at least.
Two cups at least.
Here now was the *START*.
This is us, he said.
This is us, I said.
Look for me out the Leslie Spit.
I will.
He pulled away.

⌐

I put one foot in front of the other, but it was bad as dreams.
Hardly any grab. In the shadow of these buildings. Then I
saw my uncle. He was taking film. Pumped his fist. I found
my legs. Felt the crowd. Five deep and cheering. In front
of the Hospital for Sick Children, a gaggle of Brazilians in
yellow and green saw me and went bonkers, waving their big
flag. My downtown splits were eight minutes per. I couldn't
help it. Total strangers, stretching over the barricades, telling
me way to go, wanting me to touch their hands.

⌐

At the end of University, we veered left, past the Royal York
hotel, then down and along the lake. A different city here,
all rust and blackened concrete, oil drums and cargo ships.
Not so many spectators. The stink of sewage and exhaust.
I remember a street called Cherry. Then a left on Unwin.
Thumping wind blew cold off the lake. I squinted against the
grit and tucked in back of a tall bald guy.

Making me do all the verk.

We can change it up next mile.

Stay. Vind is bitch. You are from Brazil?

No. It's my shirt.

They go crazy seeing you.

Gave me a lift.

Attention. Long vay to go.

⌐

Around the seven mile mark, we turned onto the Leslie Spit, a bare flat finger of two-lane road. Water cups rolled and skittered. A cap went wheeling past. Somebody yelled, This is fucked! Waves rammed the breakwater. BOOM, the spray blew in my eyes. Then the bald man barked in pain and hobbled off the road, clutching his cramped hamstring. I leaned into wind like a hill and remembered Calgary, where my longest run was a lazy five, every day a different mall.

⌐

Dad saw me first. He had made his turn at the end of the Spit and now was coming back the way, shouting my name, clapping hard.

That's the way, boyo! Head up, now!

In a blink he was by, but I felt brand new, fully fuelled, and started passing people. Whapped the top of the orange stanchion when I made my turn. Now the wind was at my back. It gave me a couple of freebie miles, 7:40 per. I shouted You can do it to runners still coming down the way, but not so many heard. I was still alto. A single twist of pubic hair.

About mile nine I felt my nipples, tender and raw. I tugged and tented my T-shirt. Come the eleven-mile mark, I was cursing it and wishing I had worn the Bill Rodgers singlet, its soft blue band. I poured cups of water down my neck. Then in the crowd near mile twelve, I saw a boy, older than me, with a black buzz cut and headcase grin. He said, How long did you train for this? It was odd, but I answered him. Four months. He shouted after me, You'll never make it. The breath in me fled. I stumbled. He may as well have thrown a stone, a spear, a lightning bolt. It scrambled all my circuitry. Only the foulest Glanisburgh bams would ever had said a thing like that, the dropouts and the potheads, the juvies and the brawlers. I looked back, and there he was, still leering at me. Into my head rushed all the things I could have shouted back at him. *Fuck you. Pugface. Idiot.* I told myself *settle*—a stitch coming on—and did what dad taught me, lengthened my stride, deepened my breath. Extend your wrists, breathe in. Flex your wrists, breathe out. It's a way to remind yourself. Extend, in. Flex, out. The side-stitch faded, but a sludge of fatigue was filling my legs. I had gone out too fast, and ahead of me now was the Don Valley Parkway, miles of steady, sapping incline. I looked down my T-shirt. Both nipples bled.

There were patches of autumn to the left of me, and a gigantic black-girdered bridge. Mostly I remember road. Every mile harder now than the one before. Ten yards up

and to the right, a woman in purple shorts kecked. Then it came, a stringy yellow soup, swinging from her bottom lip. She tried to keep going, but wobbled. Two volunteers ran over to catch her. I heard one say, Did you see that boy? She meant my shirt, the bloodstains. I peeled it off and kept on slogging, hoping for a second wind. Gremlins and devils and genies of pain were escaping their caves way down in my body. They gnawed and rammed. They howled. I thought to try and sing songs in my head. The only one that came to me was "Message in a Bottle." I sang it anyway.

Don Mills Road, the blue sign said. It was another turnaround point. A volunteer was gesturing like ground crew at airports. To make the hairpin round the stanchion, I had to slow right down, and very nearly stopped. Not because I thought to. My legs were giving out. My heartbeat was arrhythmic. I wondered was it possible—can someone eleven die?—but I didn't stop. I thought, Next streetlight, and made it that far.

Now, one more.

Come on.

One more.

Ahead of me, a runner laughed.

Another one said, *Look*.

I lifted my head, and blinked.

Up on the giant black-girdered bridge, a man and woman in white were waving. The woman had wings, tinfoil wings, and a big blond cloud of curls. The man held a shepherd hook and grinned through a bushy Godbeard. He pointed the hook straight at me and said something to the woman.

She blew me a kiss.

I had run under and well past the bridge before I even heard the bus.

It rolled along beside me, a boxy green-and-white old thing. In the windows, faces. I remembered some from the Leslie Spit. Then the folding doors opened. A silver-haired man stood in the stairway.

Hello, he said.

His accent was English, and his smile an effort. The eyes on him, blue inflection.

Could you board the bus, please?

No thank you. I'm fine.

Afraid you must. Regulations.

What regulations?

We're picking up the stragglers.

I'm not a straggler.

He tapped his watch. Oh yes you are.

No, I said.

Pardon me?

I have to finish.

Now, look here.

Someone on the bus said, Leave him alone.

The Englishman wagged his finger. You haven't seen the last of me, and waved the driver on.

I winced through a wall of diesel exhaust.

He picked them off one and two at a time. A few hung their heads. Others looked happy. Now the bus waited in the middle of the road.

Listen you. They have to re-open the freeway.

I pointed to the shoulder. Lots of room there.

I have strict instructions.

No.

Don't make me—

Bugger off.

Tell him, kid!

You *will* get on—

I WANT TO FINISH.

He rushed at me like a blindside flanker, but I am good at fending, and got an elbow up. BANG, right in his gob. The bus went Brazilian, and my body had wrung its adrenaline makers. I ran hard ahead and checked my shoulder, but the Englishman wasn't chasing. He was bent nearly double, face in his hands. I nearly went back to tell him sorry, but something stronger sent me on.

Here came the bus.

It passed me, doors closed.

Out an open window came a curly head. It was him with the T-shirt, *I spit left*. He gave a thumbs up, and said, Fuckin A!

I tried shouting *Stop*, but my voice was tiny.

The bus became a speck. I was out here alone.

The world disappeared. I disappeared.

Became an It.
It didn't think. It didn't run.
All It did was just not stop.
One It foot in front of the next.

He was big, noseguard big, a wide wet V on his brown T-shirt,
brown shorts too, and (I looked twice) a pair of North Stars.
Heavy pronation. The face on him red as Ragú and round.

Hi, he said

Hi.

We the last?

There was a bus.

Limey prick.

He tried to grab me.

I saw that. Nice move.

What if he comes back?

Countin on you to whup him.

What if he brings cops?

I'll tell 'em he assaulted you. Then sue his bony ass.

You're a lawyer?

Don't hold it against me.

You look like you play football.

I eat too many crullers. Christ, this is hard.

How many miles left, you think?

Five, more or less.

They took away the water.

Let's not stress the negative. What's your name?

I told him. What's yours?

Casey.

We knocked the backs of our hands together, his left hand, my right hand, and we kept on plodding. His thick upper legs along the inside were purple-red and bleeding.

—

Still with me?

Yeah.

Where you from?

Glanisburgh.

I know that town.

Pretty small.

The park.

Harris?

He nodded. Camped there once.

My dad and me do hills in it.

He in this?

I nodded ahead. Finished now.

Nice to have someone there at the end.

I said, Casey?

He said, Yeah.

I don't know if I'll make it.

Wanna stop?

No.

Okay then.

—

Ready? he asked.

You, I said.

Jeremiah. Was. Bullfrog.

Was. Good friend. Mine.

Never un'stood.

Word. He said.

Helped him.

Drink. His wine.

Always had.

Mighty. Fine wine.

We forgot the second verse, but kept on with the chorus, doing what we could with the breath we had.

Queen's Quay. Downtown was on our right. There were no more spectators, and nothing to mark the route.

Casey.

His head was lolling.

Casey. Where do we turn?

He could hardly point.

Spadina? I said.

He nodded.

The hill ahead was short but steep. Casey waved me on.

No, I said.

Can't, he said.

Casey, look at me. You have to breathe. *Look* at me.

I showed him how, the wrists.

Do it, I said. *Do* it.

Okay.

Head *up*.

Okay.

We crested the hill. He pointed right. The CN Tower. A small, dry sound escaped me.

No banner said *FINISH*. They had taken it down. The marshals had gone, the spectators. There was a line, but I ran past it, just to be sure.

Denny said, It's over, son.

I wasn't proud. I didn't care. Dad had been filming the last fifty yards. Casey told me, Go.

I pulled away from him.

He said, I'll be the one with bragging rights. Ran the Toronto Marathon. Finished absolutely last.

⌐

Dad and Denny took an arm each and helped me up the stoop. Aunty Ag gaped.

God in Heaven, son. What have they done to ye?

Away she went and had a wee greet. I gagged down electrolytes and then filled the glass with plain cold water and took it to the washroom, where Dad was slooshing Epsom salts all around the tub.

Give that a try.

Can't lift my leg.

Sit on the edge?

I tried, but could hardly bend my knees.

Right, he said. Togs off.

It embarrassed me some. My pubic hair. He pretended not to notice.

Put your arm around my neck. One, two, *hup*. Gaw you're an awful size.

He had run a marathon in three and one half hours, but

he held me, and he tilted me.

Stick your toe in. Is it too hot?

I shook my head.

He stood me in the water, and took hold of my wrists.

Lean back, he said. Go on.

Bit by bit, he lowered me in. Stripped and got in with me. Top to bottom and back again, he massaged my legs. I dunked my head and lathered with Breck.

The inside of the *Herald* building smelt like Ditto fluid. A man in an apron sent me upstairs. There was only one reporter. He was on the phone, taking notes in shorthand. An autographed photo of Stan Mikita was on the wall above his desk. Pens and pencils in a mug. An IBM Electric. He thanked the Reeve very much for his time, then hung up.

Arsewipe.

Lit a Number 7, and swivelled in his chair.

You the marathon?

Yes, I said.

Have a seat.

The story when it came out was in a box in Sports, smaller than times-table flashcards. He put in how before the race my furthest run was fifteen miles, but nothing else of what I said. Vind is bitch. Three Dog Night. That woman in purple shorts.

IT DOES NOT CONTROL YOU

Ten clicks out of Glanisburgh, he turned off River Road and drove deep into farm country, raising plumes of dust. Sunday afternoon. The car was a Gran Torino, reddish brown, a station wagon, fairly new as well. He still painted houses, but had got his EMCA badge, was full-time on the ambulance. I wore brand new Nike Stings, and he had brand new teeth, top and bottom rows, white as a fresh-flush toilet bowl.

Where we goin, Dad?

He pulled over. Out you get.

Here?

Time you learned.

To what?

Drive.

I'm fourteen.

Sooner you start.

Illegal.

Eh?

I spoke up. It's illegal.

He pointed at the empty fields. Think we'll see a copper here?

I walked round the back of the car. He walked round the front. Corn stood tall as me, bright sun, blue sky, but I was clench and goosepimples, like 10K into stiff wind on dark December mornings.

Wrong wi' you?

Nervous.

You'll be all right. Belt.

I dragged it over me, and fumbled with the clasp.

He said, Ten miles an hour. That's all it takes.

I know.

Listen. Forty and that's you through it. BANG, he thumped the windscreen. Strawberry fuckin jam o' you. First thing, always. Belt.

He taught me hands on ten and two and how to use the parking brake, then the mirrors.

Okay then, start her up.

I cranked the key—it caught—and my hands came off the steering wheel. The car felt alive and barely tame and very, very long.

Dad, I can't do this.

Can too. Hands. Right, check your blindspot.

Indicate?

Always. Foot on the brake?

42

Yes.

Yank her into Drive, then, and that's us away.

I had not been inside a church since nine years of age. It had felt like drama club, fake and rickety. Now I closed my eyes a tic, and said *GOD* to myself, then gaped at the expanse of hood, big as aircraft carriers.

Give her a bit of gas, said Dad. Easy does it. Merge.

Onto the road?

No, the ditch. Easy, easy, fucksakes. He batted my hands from the wheel. Grabbed it. Brake, he said, brake!

I stomped on the pedal like a head, and the car slid to a slanty stop—in the middle of the road.

That's you failed your Learner's, boy. Right then and there.

Three sixty-five.

Eh?

They call it a three sixty-five here.

Watch yourself.

Sorry.

Sorry isn't much good if you've fucking killed someone, is it?

No.

No. Now. Give your fucking head a shake, and get this thing pointed straight. *You* control the car. *It* does not control *you*. Sit up. Take command.

I stepped on the gas like a stair in the night, and the road cracked its knuckles underneath the rolling wheels.

That's the way, Dad said. Now, bump it up a bit.

Twenty?

Twenty-five. Go on. Now, remember. The brake is your best friend, right? If nothing else, use your brake. Minimize the impact. Take her up to thirty.

Mirage eighteen-wheelers thundered straight toward us, grilles gleaming. I wasn't cold anymore. Total opposite. Shiny-wet and slippy, the seat beneath my legs.

Not bad, kid. Thirty-five.

Thirty okay for now?

Nothing but open road up there. You're all right. Take it up.

Thirty-five felt not too bad. I gave it a little more.

Cocky now?

Back off?

More if you like.

I went forty-five.

What's that you see up ahead?

Stop sign.

Right. Start slowin up now.

I took my foot off the gas.

Brake, he said.

It's way up there.

Slow, steady pressure. Let's feel it, boy. More. More, I said. *More*.

The stop sign and the crossroads grew big in the windscreen.

Dad made a fist—BRAKE I SAID—and hammered me in the quads.

We leaned hard into our belts, and the car stopped just shy of the intersecting road, where a man with a beard in a Ford flatbed swerved to his left, and flipped us the bird.

Fuckin jerk.

Dad was gritting his freaky teeth.

When I say fucking *brake*, boy, I mean fucking BRAKE! He gave my leg another one. Hear me?

Sorry.

Listen. *You control the car*.

Okay.

Better brake too early than too bloody late. Get T-boned by that thing. He pointed at the flatbed dwindling on our right. My quad throbbed. *Back up*, he said.

Reverse?

We'll try it again. *Wait*. Check your mirrors. Okay, now. Reverse.

How far?

I'll tell you when.

Holstein cows in the field on my left had come to the fence for a look. I hated the living sight of them and craned my neck the opposite way, started backing up. A black ratsnake dragged its length from the ditch into the cornfield.

Correct, said Dad. You're drifting. Left-left-left. Brake!

We sat there and he held his face.

You flabbergast me, honestly.

Saw a snake.

Eh?

In the ditch.

Concentrate. He tapped his skull. Mind on what you're doin. We'll save reverse for later. On you go, and stop again. Six feet *back* o' the sign.

I put the car in Drive, and sped up to thirty.

Brake, said Dad. Let's *feel* it.

My whole leg and my foot twitched—to punch the gas, blow past the sign, get T-boned, be comatose—but he thumped my quad and I pressed the brake, stopped with barely a lean.

Okay, he said, and pointed left. On you go.

Main line?

Aye.

It goes to Ayrton.

So?

People will see.

Sunday afternoon? Fire a cannon down Main Street. Go on. Tallyho.

The heart in me made my T-shirt twitch, but the road was new macadam, and we were the only car. Gliding along at forty-five. Dad rolled down his window, tapped the roof, and whistled, pipes and drums, a marching tune. Wind flipped the side of his hair up and overtop, made him look way younger. Sun filled the car. It was all right, I was in control and took her up to fifty. *Ayrton*, said the sign. *5 KM.* We crested the hill by the old schoolhouse and quickly gained on a silver-blue Oldsmobile Ninety-Eight.

Dad sat up and thumped my leg. Brake, you'll be up his arse in no time. Brake, brake, brake.

The speedometer fell to thirty.

Dad said, No wonder. Look who it is.

I saw a cloud of grey-white curls, two bony hands on the wheel.

What's-her-name, Dad said. Lives on Booth in Glanisburgh. I picked up her husband last year. Heart attack.

Haig?

Aye, that's it. Silly wee thing. Shouldn't be drivin that bloody boat. He made a bullhorn of his hands. C'mon, pet. Pick it up. Right, pull out and pass.

Ayrton isn't far.

We'll be all day behind her. Check your blind spot. Indicate. Pull out and punch the gas.

I swallowed, and said, Okay.

Well?

Making sure it's clear.

Fit the *Q.E. II* in all the room you've got.

I pulled out, and floored it. The power of the car. Thirty, forty yards on, I was still in the passing lane, gripping the wheel in terror.

Foot off the gas, Dad said, and shoved his hand beneath my leg. Lifted it. Brake!

In lurching bits I steered the car back into the right lane.

Fuck was that?

You said pass.

Overtake, not blast off.

The car just went.

It did what you *made* it. Jesus H.

Can you drive now?

On into town. Right at the lights. Pull in at the IGA.

We crossed the iron swing bridge, where boat people fished for bass and perch, white buckets at their feet. The light on the other side was green. I sped up.

Easy.

The light turned yellow.

Brake.

I can make it.

Brake.

He hit my leg, and at the light, gave me another above the ear.

Round the block. Under the limit. At every red, brake.

Could use a pee.

Then get it right.

A bruise had started on my leg. By the time we got back

home, it had spread all round my birthmark. In the mirror in my room, I stared at it and thought of lies I could tell my pals about how I had got it. Dad was in the bathroom, gargling with Listermint and giving his teeth a slosh in their light blue plastic cup. Soon he was off to work, and I played *Moving Pictures* on the stereo. Lay on the rug and pressed my bruise. The harder I pressed, the more it hurt, but if I kept on pressing with my thumb, down and deeper down, it didn't hurt at all. Except when my thumb got tired, and I had to give it a rest. Then the pain flourished.

PETTY THEFT

The train sped west of urban sprawl, and I remember sunshine, a slanting, warm, and citrus light, falling on the page. I was reading Leavis, an old and forlorn copy of *The Great Tradition*. Thin, brittle pages came loose as I turned them, and ink smudged my fingertips. I got up to go and wash, but heard footfalls behind me. High-voltage panic hummed in my chest, and the conductor said, "Excuse me, sir," on his brisk way by. He was a stout and ruddy Scot, severe and sergeant-major-ish. Spun on his heel at the front of the car and asked for our attention. "On behalf of VIA Rail, I apologize sincerely for the failing ventilation. It will be serviced in Waterloo, during a short delay." With that, he spun on his heel again and moved through the vestibule with practised surety.

I had noticed nothing wrong, despite my heavy woolen suit, but a cramp had started in my neck. It happens when I read. As the train began to brake, I stood in the aisle to stretch a bit and stole another look at the attractive older woman. She was on the aisle, one across and down from me, fanning her fine, intelligent face with a folded *Globe and Mail*. Great skin. Athletic calves. A fancy leather briefcase stood on the seat beside her. Lawyer, I guessed. Or CFO. Possibly a prof. I imagined myself older and having kids with her, a Tudor house and a dog and car. What all that would be like. At which point she looked at me, as if to say, "Do you mind?" I made for the exit, feeling dumb and itchy in my out-of-season tweed.

The suit was three years old now. I had worn it twice, the first time at my high school grad, then in court in Peterborough, when I was convicted. That was seven months ago, and though I still made Dean's List, not a day went by without suffering in my head the bite-and-grip of handcuffs, the ritual diminishment of mugshots and prints, then the dreary theatre of entering a plea. "I am contemplating Law, Your Honour." That's what I told the judge. Crying like a kid. One of the townie troglodytes waiting his turn behind me sniggered with a friend. The judge threw him a look, and I bleated on. "No one knows more than I how foolish this was." That sort of thing. I had stolen acne cream: Benzagel, high-end stuff, seven bucks a tube. "I can only hope, Your Honour, my actions will not ruin me." He scratched his beard and stared at me over his bifocals, then bestowed a conditional discharge.

My criminal record would be erased after six months' probation and twenty-four hours' community service—painting fire hydrants, I thought, or picking up litter in city parks. But, for half a dozen weekends, I reported to the Peterborough Y and played dodge ball with latchkey kids. There were field trips, too, singalongs on school buses to and from the Science Centre, Queen's Park, and the ROM. I had never been to places like those, and I saw how happy the kids could be.

Still, you don't feel discharged. You feel conditional. Perpetually detected.

Inside the station, I passed a bank of payphones and ogled the concession stand: ham and cheese, turkey-swiss, egg salad, hot dogs. The smell made me nuts, and I felt in my breast pocket the obscene redundancy of a brand new leather billfold. I had bought it yesterday at Cunningham and Smythe. The owner even remembered me. Soon as I walked in, he said, "Donegal tweed, charcoal grey." I grinned. "How is your dad?"

"Fine," I said, "fine."

"What can I help you with today?"

I told him I was thinking of a spring/summer suit, which was more or less true, 'til I saw how much. "Sorry," was all I had to say, "think I've changed my mind," but I let the owner shadow me. "Italian linen, sir." He slipped jacket after jacket over my sloped shoulders. I pretended none of them were quite what I was looking for and finally bought a shirt.

Even had him steam it. "Certainly, sir. No problem, sir." At the checkout counter, thumbing through the last of my little bursary, I tapped the glass and said, "I'll take the billfold, there." He asked me was I sure. I nodded aristocratically. Twenty ham and cheese was what that fucker cost, even more egg salad, as though cordovan leather would prove to my sister I was doing ticketyboo.

She was nine years older and had gone with Mum to Calgary back in '75 or so. In '79, she married Tim, a tier-two defenceman who never made pro, but his father owned a PetroCan, and Janice did the books. For most of the eighties, business was bad, but picking up now, and they needed help. I wasn't big on pumping gas, but couldn't face another year of drop sheets and my dad. He and his last girlfriend had gone south pretty ugly. Bottles of British Navy Rum heaped in his bin. He spent most of every night yelling at the news, declaiming sundry hatreds. To suburban housewives who changed their minds about the trim, he said, "Yes, of course, ma'am." Called them cunts when they had gone. Charged twelve an hour like it was just deserts. Tim and Janice were paying me nine. Dad would understand that, is what I told myself, staring at those payphones. I promised I would write him, then spent all my pocket change on a day-old bagel. Wolfed both halves.

A big-bellied man with curly white hair was sitting beside the older woman, chomping a wad of purple gum and reading *The Bourne Identity*. I thought, What a dick, and opened *The Great Tradition*. A few minutes later, when the train had achieved full speed, someone behind me belched and said, "Beg your pardon." Then he all but fell into the seat beside me. The left sleeve of his Argos coat was torn cuff to shoulder. He took off his tinted glasses and held them in front of his weathered face, blinking, wobbly-headed. I tried to keep on reading, but felt him looking at the page.

"Fuck," he said, "is that?"

I showed him the cover.

He shook his head. "Christ." Then said, "No offence," and offered his hand. "Bob."

His grip was limp and clammy. I tried to read again.

He said, "Where you headed?"

I said, "Out west."

"Student?"

I told him I went to Queen's, and he said, "Used to teach there."

I gaped at him. "English?"

"Fuck no. Economics. Then I moved. Waterloo."

"You teach there now."

"Did."

"Retired?"

"No. I told 'em, 'It's all a crock a shit.'"

"What is?"

"Economics."

"You said that?"

"Yup."

"To who?"

"Fuck you think? My students."

I turned in my seat to face him. "Are you kidding me?"

"Nope."

"You really said that. 'A crock of shit.'"

"'Get out a here. Go live.'"

"What happened?"

"Sat there, most of 'em. Stunned fucks. I walked out."

"You just left?"

"Gone."

"That's just . . . it?"

He checked his watch. "Come have a drink."

"Early for me."

"Just the one."

I glanced at my book and felt the billfold graze my ribs.

He said, "It's on me."

"Just the one."

"Atta boy."

The attractive older woman was reading her newspaper and did not look up on our way by. Fuckface with the gum did, signalling his disgust with the likes of Bob, who failed to notice or to care. He had a scab big as a nickel in the middle of his bald spot, and what with his coat and grubby shoes, I thought some pince-nez maître d' would tut and turn us both away. I had never been in a club car before and was picturing chandeliers. Maybe you get those in first class. This was more like an upstairs lounge in a small-town hockey rink—tin ashtrays and bad teeth, ball caps and back fat. Bob got in line at the bar, and I found a table. Three men beside me drank rye and Coke and talked about a black bear one of them had shot. A kink started in my calf. I was clenching that much. Hated this and wanted out, but Bob sat down with tins of Blue and plastic cups stuck on top. We poured, and his hand shook.

I said, "So, what's next for you?"

"Depends on my divorce."

"Sorry."

He said, "Don't be," and lit a Player's Light. "Been up to Manitoulin?"

"No. Hear it's nice."

"Friend a mine has a cabin there. Think I'll hole up."

"Sounds like a plan."

"Stay hosed a month. Maybe fish some walleye. Ever fish walleye?"

"Not really my thing."

"You're twenty-what?"

"One."

"Payin a bunch a peckerheads to tell you what to read."

"Maybe I like it."

"Why?"

"Heard Economics was a crock."

"Hardy-har. Why."

I began a breathless homily. Most of it was stolen straight out of Leavis or what my profs had said. Literature improves the mind, refines the soul, increases human sympathy.

Bob was staring at me over his tinted glasses. The whites of his eyes made me think of eggs on the fry in a diner. He waved down the barman and said, "Hell of a speech, kid. Shit costs you what these days, three, four grand a year?"

I shrugged, "'Bout that."

"Loans?"

I told him, "Some."

"Well. Hope the tail is good."

I said, "I get my share."

"Sure, kid. Bet you do."

The barman had arrived. He was big and ginger-haired and did not look impressed. I sat up straight, displaying my sobriety and fine, tailored tweed. He set down two more

Blue, and Bob tipped him three bucks, then lit another cigarette. I slid my second tin across.

"What the fuck."

"I said just the one."

"Loosen up."

"I'm good, thanks."

"Fuck's with you young guys today? When did you get so well behaved?"

I stared out the window.

"Your age, I was in Africa."

"Congrats. I'm not you."

"Listen to me a minute."

I told him, "Go ahead."

He started in on Bobo profs and higher-ed as mind control. *Theory of the Leisure Class*. Weber and Marcuse. He said I would be thirty and in shitheaps of debt. Half my life paying down my own indoctrination. By now he was on his third beer. Began to slur his words—*state apparati, reification*. He signalled the barman and gassed on. I hid away inside myself. Had done the same with my old man a hundred, hundred times: Culloden (yet again), Thatcher, JFK, Caribbeans, homosexuals. Whatever it is, let him talk. Eventually, it stops.

The barman picked our empties up, and Bob said, "*Un autre.*"

"I think it is better coffee. Or maybe water. Soft drink."

"C'mon, big guy."

"Sorry."

"Piece a shit."

The barman slapped down his tray. Dregs splashed my shirt. He jabbed a finger at Bob and me. "You want," he said, "to stay on the train?"

I said, "Fuck did I do?" and gestured at my shirt.

"Out, now. Both of you."

Heads had turned. Someone laughed.

Bob stood, swaying, and I followed him out. The motion of the train made him stagger that much more. By the washroom, he lurched, and when I tried to steady him, he yanked his arm away.

"Fuck off, kid."

"Suit yourself."

He locked the washroom door and began hacking terribly. I said, "You okay in there?" but he didn't answer.

Back in my seat, I tongue-dabbed my finger and rubbed at the stains on my forty-dollar shirt. Became increasingly murderous, and rehearsed several fights with the frogfuck barman. A fistful of his ginger hair, slamming his face over and over into the tabletop. After that, I thought up furious letters to the head of VIA Rail. Checked my shoulder now and then, but no sign of Bob. The attractive older woman had struck up a conversation with the big-bellied man. I decided she was a philistine too, and tried to read *The Great Tradition*, but my weight that year had dropped below a hundred and sixty pounds (I am pushing six foot five), and beer in the early afternoon always conked me out.

I woke having dreamt I was late for the train.

A man beside me said, "G'day."

He was gaunt and badly pockmarked, with a handlebar mustache, and black gaps in his grin. With a total hoser accent, and overdone politeness, he said, "Name's Joe. Just got on in Parry Sound." Stuck out his grimy mitt. When we shook, he switched his grip to the macho kind. I wanted to go and wash my hand.

He said, "Where you headin?"

I said, "Calgary."

He looked at me like fame, and leaned into the aisle, telling nearby passengers, "Man's goin west." Shook my hand again, "Honour to fuckin meet you," then reached inside his denim coat and offered me the bottle, its green neck protruding from a brown paper bag.

I waved it off.

"Primes the pump."

"Maybe later."

He sucked the pungent stuff back in eye-popping quantity. The big-bellied man issued a snort, and the Scots conductor came through, calling, "Tickets, please." Joe hid his bottle and dragged a hand across his mouth.

"Well, look who it is."

"How she goin, guy?"

"Can't complain, Joe."

"Got 'er right here."

"Have you now?"

"Paid for." Joe produced a ticket. "Sudbury."

"I see that."

"Got myself a squaw."

"Did you?"

"Beauty."

"I'm sure she's a keeper. Behave yourself, now."

The conductor moved on, and grinning Joe jerked his thumb. "Knows me."

I said something like "Mm."

"Don't put up with no shit, neither."

"I imagine not."

Minutes passed. I tried to read, but Joe bobbed his knee, and out came the bottle. "Coast is clear, Cochise."

"You go ahead."

"C'mon, get 'er in you. She's a long fuckin ride."

I smelled the rim. "What is this?"

"Lemon gin. The good stuff."

I swallowed a bitter thimbleful.

Joe had another walloping slug, and slid the paper bag down. "Best save some for my honey."

I said, "Good idea."

"She can fuckin go." He nudged me in the ribs. "Ever had the red meat?"

"No."

"Could set you up with some."

"I'll keep it mind, thanks."

He nudged me again, and I pictured hitting him, but stared out the window, aware of his knee. Daylight was fading. I remember islands, small rocky islands, little Group of Seven things, out in Georgian Bay—at least I thought it was Georgian Bay—I had never been this far by land. Joe introduced himself to surrounding passengers, telling every one of them he had just got on in Parry Sound, asking where they were headed. Nobody replied. "Friendly bunch," Joe said. Reclined his seat, "Fuck yous, then," and soon was sawing logs. His mouth sagged crookedly, revealing black-rot stumpy teeth and ulcerating gums. I looked up and down the length of the car, but every seat was taken. His snoring was incredible. It hit every ugly note, hissing sibilants, clicks and smacks, long, whistling fricatives. The bottle of lemon gin was forever leaning, threatening to tip. I righted it. It leaned again. I righted it. It leaned again. On and on like this through distended minutes. I was getting hungry and berated my lack of self-control. Wolfing that bagel. Should have saved half. I had thirty-seven dollars left and forty-odd more hours between here and Calgary. Other passengers had brought their own food. I had brought F.R. Leavis, and when the sandwich cart came through, dropped four eighty-five on a turkey-swiss. The transaction woke Joe. His eyes were twin catastrophes, gunky and bloodshot.

"Got there, Kemo Sabe?"

I just kept chewing. It was cold and stale with too much butter.

Joe discovered his bottle. Had himself a haul. Offered me it.

"No."

"Maybe I'll just finish 'er off."

"You go right ahead."

"I can go all night on this stuff. Never blow my load."

He twisted in his seat, and had a long filthy look at the older woman.

"What do you think a that?"

"Think she's a little rich for you."

"Throw a solid fuck in her." His elbow in my ribs. "I would too. In the washroom, eh?"

He cupped his hands around an imaginary ass, and began to thrust. The bottle tipped. I shot up.

He leaned back, wincing at me through his fingers. "Fuck you doin?"

"Shut *up*."

I had cocked a fist and stood over him a moment more, hot in the face, racing heart. My trouser leg wet with gin. Then I pounded up the aisle, Joe swearing after me, and locked the washroom door. Someone must have just been in for a monstrous shit. I had to hold my breath. Water puddled and ran on the floor and sloshed in the little sink. I drained it and dampened a paper towel. Dabbed my trouser leg. There was piss on and around the toilet seat. Sodden Kleenex and toilet paper lay on the floor like dead and wounded. The stink was not abating. I didn't want to go sit down, but couldn't stay in here, and thought of maybe standing in the vestibule. Which is when I heard the connecting doors, then the conductor and the big-bellied man.

"Guy's a menace."

"I'll see to it, sir."

Their voices faded up the aisle. I opened the bathroom door a bit. A shouting match was on.

The train began slowing down. I stayed where I was until it had stopped. Up at the front of the car, Joe wrenched his arm free from the conductor's grip.

"Fuckin touch me!"

"Joe, take a telling. Out now, or it's coppers."

"My fuckin money back!"

"I'll get you on the next train. Once you've calmed down."

"What about my woman!"

"She'll have to wait."

Joe stared daggers at me. "Fuck you lookin at!"

"Sir," said the conductor, "could you resume your seat, please."

"Is there anything I can do?" I said.

"Sir. Resume your seat."

I watched out the window. Joe let himself be led across the narrow platform and into the little station. Soon the conductor was back on board, and seemed to me rather pleased with himself, as though he had just finished an invigorating run. He apologized for the delay and started down the aisle. I readied explanations, but he only winked on his way by and gave the all-clear on his walkie-talkie. The train pulled away, and the empty bottle of lemon gin rolled from beneath the seat in front. I set my foot on top of it. Ontario went on.

I slept again, but fitfully, and woke in a sweat, wrenching my left arm away from a phantom grip. Here and there a reading light. Otherwise, the car was dark. I took off my blazer and folded it in half on the empty seat. One across and down, the attractive older woman dozed, her head leaning to the right, then resting on the shoulder of the big-bellied man, who levelled a kingshit look at me. I stretched my arms and neck. On a tall smokestack in the near distance, aircraft warning lights blinked like Christmas. The conductor thumped and swished up the aisle. "Sudbury, ten minutes." Then the overhead lights blinked on. I thumbed through the mustiness of my F.R. Leavis. *Adam Bede*, *Nostromo*, *The Portrait of a Lady*. I was reading *about* these books before I had read the books themselves. Often that got me by in school, where you didn't need to *be* well read. You just had to sound it.

I shoved *The Great Tradition* down deep into the seat pocket, and resolved to stop play-acting, in school and the rest of life. Be upfront and honest. It would start in Calgary. I was going to sit my sister down and tell her what had happened. A tube of pimple cream. She would understand. We might even laugh. I had learned my lesson, I had worked with kids, still made the Dean's List, and was doing all right. I told myself that, may even have said it out loud, "You're doing all right." Then I saw the girl, waiting on the platform at Sudbury station, thin, bare arms folded across her chest. She had high heel boots on, and torn fishnet stockings. A black tank top, and cleavage. Danger in those feral eyes. Danger, danger, danger.

She got on near the front of the train, but by the time it left Sudbury, had worked her way down. I grabbed *The Great Tradition* and pretended to read. Arms still held in that pale X, she stopped by the aisle seat and looked at my jacket, then at me. I remember her small knees and the bad, girly perfume.

"Hey."

I ignored her.

"Hey. Can I sit here?"

She looked maybe grade ten and sounded drunk or stoned or both.

"Please, can I sit here?"

I kept my eyes averted, and reached for my blazer.

"Thanks."

I turned toward the window and draped the blazer over me, faking easy sleep. An eastbound freight train blasted by only a couple yards away. I watched the passing blur of it, and when it was gone, saw her in the darkened glass, facing me, watching me.

She said, "I'm goin to Dryden."

I closed my eyes again.

"Gonna see Dave."

Kept them closed.

"He likes me. He'll take care a me."

Long moments passed.

"You're not really sleepin."

I opened my eyes and turned to her. "Could you be quiet, please?"

She said, "What's your name?"

"You want to know my name."

"Yeah."

I told her one. "What's yours?"

She paused and said, "Ruby."

Her lips were big and glossy. A large oval tear in the fishnet on her thigh. She said, "I'm goin to Dryden."

"You already told me that."

"Can you lend me twenty dollars?"

"I don't have twenty dollars."

She said, "I ran away."

"From home?"

"I used a piece a glass," she said, and then showed me her right forearm. A vicious red runnel ran the inside length of it.

"You have to go to the hospital."

"Where I ran away from."

"Why?"

"Get away from Wayne and Wanda."

"Your mom and dad?"

"Foster parents. They give us drugs. They do. Even the little kids, so they stay asleep."

"Call the police."

"Dave said I could live with him. Long as I want."

Through the connecting doors up front I saw the conductor. He had paused to punch a ticket, but was headed this way.

"Please, mister. Twenty bucks."

"I can't."

"He'll kick me off this train."

"He can get you help."

She leaned close, and whispered, "You can fuck my mouth."

Usually what I say is I hid out in the washroom, but that isn't true. I waited for her there. I left the door unlocked, and I pictured it, getting mouthfucked by a kid amidst that stink and squalor. When I heard her footfalls a couple minutes later, I slid the lock across, but it was no big moral thing. I was scared, that's all. Maybe I mean terrified. Anyway, when I came out, the train had begun to slow down, and the girl had gone. Shamefaced and sweaty, I went back to my seat. Another measly station in another measly town. The car doors opened, admitting nighttime air.

I had my blazer halfway on when I felt the absent weight. Clutched all its pockets. Looked beneath the seat. My face was hot like scalding, and I went numb, rigid. It was like last fall outside Shoppers Drug Mart, when the store detective grabbed my arm. Glee lit up his little rat-face, and a small jewel twinkled in his left ear. He nodded at the pocket of my denim coat and asked what I had in it. I answered him. I told him he had caught me. I even called him sir.

DOGSHIT BLUES

His second call came within a minute of the first. I said hello and waited. From the dregs of himself, he mustered speech.

Son.

Yes.

Your nana.

I know. Dad, you told me. You just called, and told me.

Slow, appalling seconds passed.

Son.

Yes.

Your nana.

Dad . . .

I drew a drape—wet snow—and pressed my headache, hard.

Are you still at the place on Naseby?

He made a sound like yes.

Stay where you are. I'm out the door. Dad, do you hear me?

I ran up Division, past the Hoagie House. An emaciated teen shoved her bawling baby in a stroller through the slush. My wrists were cold. I hate that. Puddles ankle deep. Near Regiopolis-Notre Dame, a city bus lumbered by, heaving the horrible weight of itself. I should have flagged it down. Division is bitching long. The harder I ran the longer it got. Intersections multiplied. Division and Kirkpatrick. Division and Elliot. These streets were strange and mocking me. I stopped and walked and went inside a shabby Esso station. The clerk looked warm in her red fleece, eating ketchup chips.

Loonie and four quarters, please.

Her mouth postponed its chewing.

Sorry. Can't make change.

My hair and most of the rest of me dripped.

I need to get a bus.

Sorry. Not allowed.

I looked at the pepperoni sticks.

How much?

Forty cents.

I fished one out. She brushed crumbs and ketchup dust off her porky fingers.

Know when the next one is? I said.

She said, What.

Bus.

Depends.

On what.

Which bus.

Whichever one goes *that* way.

I don't know. Soon.

I took my change.

Thanks.

Forgot your pepperoni, guy.

I went back for it. She pointed past me bug-eyed.

There it is now, she said.

I ran full tilt and hollered. In the back window, two boys watched. The one in the Boston Bruins toque lit right up and cheered me. I shouted, Tell the driver. Tell the driver, stop! The kid looked up the aisle. Then he looked back at me. A ferrety little grin. As the bus pulled farther away, he took off his glove and made a fist. At its base, he turned an imaginary crank. Slowly, his middle finger stood. I threw the pepperoni stick. End over end like fetch it went. Way wide of the bus. I stopped and bent and breathed, spat. Should have worn runners. These old soaking Docs, the clumsy thick-heeled weight of them. A corn on my fourth toe. Anyway, I kept on. It was one thing I was good at.

Watching out for coppers, I stood this side of the 401 and wore a bemused-embarrassed look, as though I had never hitched in my life and only had to do so now out of would-you-believe-it circumstance. Maybe a hundred cars went by. Then a hundred more. The looks you get. The looks you don't. I recited Wallace Stevens and alternated thumbs. Spattered minutes dragged. Arby's smelled delicious, Wendy's, KFC. I craved a stack of greasy meat and began to glare at drivers. A minivan or K-car got the whole of my attention, as though I could brake the vehicle and predispose its driver through Jedi-like mind-tricks. Snow splatted on windshields. My overcoat held a weight of wet. Come on, I said. I'm not a bum. I go to Queen's, hear me? That's right, you asshole. Don't even blink. Have a nice day. How 'bout you? We could chat. I'll be anyone you like. Will no one fucking stop for me?

Somebody.

You.

Please.

~

Metallica rattled the body and glass of a white Hyundai Pony. One of its headlights shone. The driver had chops and long black hair, a tank top in November. He was wide as one and a half of me, big arms all tattoo. I dropped my thumb and wished him on. Then his blinker flashed, and the clanking heap pulled over, coughing dark exhaust.

Comin or not? I gotta jet.

A Marshall amp and guitar case took up most of the small back seat. I got in the front and gaped at road through a hole in the floor, big as a medium pizza.

He said, Keep your feet up.

Checked his shoulder. Merged.

Far you headed?

I nearly told him Napanee, but pushed my luck.

Belleville.

Like heavy metal?

I said, Fuckin eh.

He cranked up *Ride the Lightning*. *H-A-T-E*, his right-hand knuckles said. I looked for a seat belt. He yelled, It's broke, and stomped the gas. At ninety clicks, the Pony shook. He went *woo-woo* like Indians, and when he laughed, I saw his gums, the pits and ulcerations.

What's your name?

I told him one.

He whapped his chest.

Wade.

A black knight with a battle-axe was vivid on his bicep.

I said, Frank Frazetta?

He said, Fuckin rights, and we shook like bikers.

Smoke?

I said, Sure.

They were Export 'A.' The Greens. It was like inhaling a shotgun blast.

He said, You all right?

Yeah.

I watched a blur of 401 between my aching legs. He jerked his thumb toward the back.

I got chicken. Have some.

The bag was behind his seat. It was Mary Brown's.

He said, Take the breast.

Sure?

Yeah. I like the leg.

The box was warm in my hands, and it came with taters. He turned off the stereo.

You sure you're all right?

I said my dad was pretty sick.

Shoulda fuckin told me. This cunt'll do one-forty.

⟶

I think he would have driven me the whole way if I asked. But amputated feet, my windshield-shredded face—I kept on seeing these—and wreckage, jaws of life. A friend is meeting me, I said. At the Quinte Mall. He wished me luck with my old man.

I watched him pull a U-ey, then turned and started humping it up Highway 62. A dead cat lay on its side in the ditch. Toward it hopped a crow.

I ran another hundred yards. Here came an eighteen-wheeler. I made plenty of room for it, but the driver grinned and signalled me.

Where you go?

Glanisburgh.

This is luck. I go there.

He was a small and pointy man with bristly ginger hair. In his close-together eyes, happy devils danced.

Thanks for this, I said.

Is no problem for me.

He got the big truck rolling and pointed at a gym bag on the seat between us.

Towel, he said.

Sorry.

What can you do? Shitty day.

I dried my hair and face and neck. The cab was warm and very clean.

He said, You live Glanisburgh?

Grew up there. Kingston now.

I deliver IGA.

In Glanisburgh? There isn't one.

MacMillan Family IGA.

Since when?

I don't know. For me, always.

They used to be independent. Back when I worked there.

Now you are the student?

I said, Supposed to be.

Mathematic? Physic?

No, I said. English.

Shakespeare, Milton, Hardy.

Yeah, all of that.

Who is your prefer?

I don't know. It changes. I guess Samuel Beckett.

En Attendant Godot! he said. Do you speak the French?

A bit.

Moi, je m'appelle Zibby.

That short for Zbigniew?

Your pronounce is good.

Where are you from?

Poland.

I mean which part.

Krakow.

Beautiful, I said.

Yes. You go there?

No. I've seen pictures.

He nodded and didn't speak again until we passed Oak Hills. Then he asked if I like Bach. The only Bach I had ever heard was in a film about Glenn Gould, but I told him yes. He pushed a cassette into the slot, and turned it up.

Cello?

My instrument, he said.

You can play this?

He looked along the road, and shrugged.

Poland, I am cello. Canada, drive truck.

Adrenaline, cortisol, tension in the neck: getting close to Glanisburgh always threw my panic switch, but the music calmed me some, and we shared his Thermos, a berry-flavoured tea.

Pelting past St. Andrew's church I pitched and fell in slush. Got up dripping rage. Every time I left this town, I swore it was my last. Tight-lipped, pale, pinched people. The pool hall. Giant Tiger. My father had left Scotland for its dull, dull-witted mimicry.

He lived in an addition on the back of a two-storey red-brick house. White vinyl siding. A semi-covered stoop. The yellow-orange bowl was there. It brimmed with dirty melt, which I flung beneath the spruce. For a while, I stared at the chewed-through lead, still dangling from the clothesline, and swallowed a wad of clog in my throat. He may as well have starved the thing. Huskies need to run. I took a breath and squared myself. The heart in me was thumping. At the least I could wash and dry my clothes. If his electric wasn't cut off. A decent bite to eat.

He was never one to lock the door. I wrenched and shoved, knocked and called. Checked beneath his mat. Then in his glutted mailbox. He still subscribed to *Runner's World*. Bills said *Final Notice*. Round the back I made slush balls, splatted his bedroom window. A crowbar in the back of his van, but it was shut up tight. Out front, I banged on his landlady's door. Rang the bell. A curtain twitched. I think it twitched. Anyone looking out would have seen a soggy, frantic, lanky man yelling Hello and Help me and, finally, You fuck. I looked up and down the empty street. An impotence of wet-black trees. Drab hills in the distance. It put a grim resolve in me. A slablike sense of duty.

Back at his stoop, I used a stone to brace the screen wide open and then stepped back ten feet or so. In Cyprus, he and his section had raided suspect homes. His job was the door, and on many a rum-stoked night, he described how. Get a running start. Lean into the kick. You want your weight behind it. Plant the heel of your boot as close to the lock as possible. Think *through* the door.

Wood and metal pieces flew, hit the fridge, and fell. I gaped at my achievement—the busted hinge, the splintered jamb—and for a moment I was proud, felt the height and weight of me. Then I looked around.

A stack of Molson Ex in twelves climbed the side of his grungy stove. Forties of amber rum, all but one of them empty, stood amidst a slew of mail on the kitchen table. Squished tea bags and spare-rib bones brimmed his stinking garbage bin. A slaw of vomit glistened on a white spaghetti strainer in the piled, bristling sink. Standing there, I called to him. Enormous silence answered. I checked the living room. Over in the corner, aged grey turds crumbled on the shag.

At the foot of the stairs, I called again and willed him to appear, shaved and dressed, suitcase in hand, berating the filthy state of me. He did not appear, and I went up one stair at a time, calling him still, feebly. His bedroom door was shut. I stood before it shaking. Graphic scenes assailed me. Belt. Or borrowed sawed-off. His finely stropped straight razor. One more time I called him, and went in like I used to, as though it were Sunday morning, and I had made him his cup of tea. The room was dark. I felt for a switch.

Amidst a thrown-off twist of sheets, he lay naked on his back, head leaning slightly this way, bottom dentures jutting. He was ashen, and his eyes had shut. Residue glazed his chin. He knew all the docs in town. To get a scrip would be easy.

I honestly thought to thump him. Thick, dull thump of stiff dead flesh. Instead, I blubbered and knelt at his feet, held them, and rubbed his calluses. Breath crackled in his throat. I recoiled and smacked my head against the windowsill. Dad, I said. His eyelid twitched. Scrambling up, I found his pulse. Dad, can you hear me? Both his eyelids fluttered. I slapped his stubbled face. He made a small and strangled sound. Give us your teeth, I said, working them out and setting them by *Glencoe* on his nightstand. Have you taken something? Dad, it's me. Listen. His eyes opened, blankly stared, then consciousness filtered into them, and he worked his shrunken mouth. Son. I got hold of a wrist and pulled. Up he came. Can you sit? He nodded, but barely, and tugged at the sheet, covering his groin, breathing shallow, fitful breaths, his greasy, grizzled hair deranged. Hard men once had feared him. He managed a look at me.

What is it you're doin home?

You called me. Twice. Do you not remember?

I watched his rum-sluggish circuitry work.

Mum, was all he said.

I'm sorry, Dad. I am.

We sat for a while.

Time is it?

Don't know, I said. Afternoon.

Monday.

No Dad. Tuesday.

I watched the wobbly up-and-down of his knobby Adam's apple.

Do you need to be sick?

No.

He turned his head away.

I said, Can you manage tea?

His voice cracked. Good idea.

I made room in the wretched sink and got the kettle on. A stain on his sofa smelt of piss. I sat on the floor at this end of the coffee table strewn with old photographs, most of me and the dog, a few of Dad and Nana. I hadn't known her well, and my American Poetry midterm was at nine tomorrow. I needed to be fresh and have exact quotations at my fingertips. Upstairs, the toilet seat slapped against the tank, and Dad fell to his knees. He would not be having tea. I unplugged the kettle and got stuck in on clean-up, reciting lines from Ezra Pound, *Hugh Selwyn Mauberley*. Dog shit powdered in my grasp.

PRIVATE FUNCTION

In her cramped Alberta kitchen, Janice said, "Serviettes," said it flatly, to herself, opening a cupboard. I watched her from a La-Z-Boy in the sitting room. She had taken up swimming, and was thinking of a mini-tri in B.C. in the spring. To me, she looked less fit than wiry and bleached. Most of the colour in her face had been brush applied. Greenish hues iridesced in her split and frizzy highlights. I un-reclined the chair and said, "Tell me what to do." She answered in the same flat voice. "You could hit my husband."

Over on the chesterfield, Tim in mesomorphic ease turned a page of *Water Ski*. "Barefoot boom," was all he said, then his semivacant gaze drifted back to the bigscreen Sony, where the puzzle was a phrase, and Vanna turned an *M*. Beth, meanwhile, my youngest niece, eight years old next month, sat amidst the Hoover marks, making Ken and Barbie dolls coo in French immersion. I looked at the VCR—7:23. A bilge of lasagna and boxed cab sauv shifted in my belly. Janice said, "Dessert forks," and nine-year-old Glenny, bigger than most kids her age, lolloped down the hall. Clapping the cordless back in its base, she solved the *Wheel of Fortune* puzzle, "'X MARKS THE SPOT'!" at a single glance, then told Tim, "Go help Mom." He thumbed the remote, hard. Beth poked POWER on the set, and mimed retardation.

"Change the thtoopid battery."

"Why don't you be nice?"

"*Told* you a thousand times."

Further fracas happened, and Janice bared her teeth. "COULD we please PRETEND?"

I fucked off to the big front room. It was hardly ever used, though they put the tree there, and I took some *Wish Book* solace in its lovely, blinking glow. Maybe an easeful minute passed. I forgot my troubled stomach. Then behind me Beth said, "*Boo*," and ran to the picture window, where she whacked the hanging blinds apart.

Janice called, "Them?"

Beth said, "Yep," and grinned at me in headlight glare.

I said, "Go away."

She sneered at me. "My house."

I tried again. "Please."

On her way by, she made a fist and thumped my upper leg, but I was alone again and peered between the blinds. A new-looking Oldsmobile Ninety-Eight Regency Brougham had come to a stop by the snow-covered curb.

Mum went round to the driver side and helped him out, steadied him. I couldn't really see his face (he wore a winter trilby, and his head was down) but he walked like what he was: an old and brittle man. Also my next stepdad. His name was Jack DeWitt.

Back in the sitting room, Tim knelt at the fireplace and lit an artificial log. Cold air had wafted in from the vestibule, where Janice and the girls were greeting Mum and Jack. I stayed out of sight, listening to their voices.

"New coat, Mum?"

"Marks and Sparks. How are my little loves?"

"Fine, Grandma. You look nice."

"Let me see your hands."

"JACK," said Janice. "How are YOU?"

"Minus twenty-eight."

"She's asking how you ARE," said Mum.

Jack said, "Oldsmobile."

Tim saw me grimace. "Told you so," he said.

Clutching a double handful each of Devon butter toffees, Beth and Glenny scampered up the set of stairs from the vestibule, and gleamed with canny schadenfreude as soon as they saw my fallen face. I feigned nonchalance, an adult self-sufficiency, but wanted to wound the little shits. Giggle, giggle, giggle. "Girls, cool it," Tim said, spooning Suisse Mocha mix into Christmas mugs. The kettle had just boiled. I said, "Bailey's—lots in mine," and Mum made her entrance, smelling of Chanel.

I had seen her four times in sixteen years and often lived

as though she were dead. Now here she was, incontrovertible, opening her arms. Maybe she felt the normal things. Filial love, all that. Maybe I did too. Anyway, I kissed her cheek and told her she looked smashing. That much was true. Mum's thing for kitsch—slasher films, bingo halls, Foody Goody, Vegas—did not extend to fashion. She had on a matching black jacket and skirt, and the latest do was high-glam, short and dyed a brassy blond.

"You've put on weight," she said.

Tim gripped my bicep. "All that iron he's been pumpin. Special coffee, Viv?"

"Love one, thanks. I'm frozen."

"What about your man?"

"A glass of tepid water, Tim." She turned toward the vestibule "JACK? Are you coming?"

Like a cheery physiotherapist, Janice said, "Almost there!"

I looked at Beth and Glenny, their eyes alight with feral glee, and then he *eked* into the room, thin as ethnic cleansing. Three stairs had walloped him. He stood sag-mouthed and wheezing. Snot glazed the middle of his grizzled little mustache. His gunky eyes bulged at me.

Mum said, "Darling, this is my SON."

His bony hand still had some grip, and he said, "It's an HONOUR," as though I were an earl, or some kind of dignitary, a top hat on whose behalf he had sailed to far-flung tropics, returning a ravaged wreck of a man, still somehow in thrall to dank codes of honour. It baffled me, but I felt myself adopting the same bizarre solemnity, the same shrinking deference.

"Sir," I said, hand on heart, "the honour is all MINE."

Janice gaped at this exchange. Desperately, I looked to her. She said in her having-visitors voice, "Who's having cake?"

Though I sat as far away from Jack as the room allowed, up at the end of the chesterfield, closest to the hall, I couldn't help but look at him, like carnage on a highway. Throughout ice-breaking chit-chat, he sat there barely breathing, hand trembling to and fro between his blazer pocket and his bony, jutting knee. Glenny and Beth, cross-legged on the floor a few feet in front of me, nudged each other, loving this. Janice gave them a cutting look, then asked Mum if she and Jack had found a mobile home yet.

"We have," said Mum. "A double-wide." She looked at Jack. "Our lot as well."

He said, "Eh?"

"Our lovely LOT."

He grunted something like a yes and dragged a hanky from his pants.

Janice leaned toward him. "Will you miss the LODGE?"

He gave his snoot a long wet honk, nodded, and said, "Good people."

"Loves his euchre," Mum said, opening her purse.

Jack came to sudden life, producing as if by magic a silver-plated Zippo. After lighting Mum's Dunhill, he took from his shirt pocket a pack of Export 'A'—Green. I had smoked a Green once. It almost made me puke, but Jack puffed away like a bogman Bond, and Mum said to me, "How is school, dear?"

"Between bad and awful."

She tutted and turned to Jack. "He won a scholarship."

"What's that?"

"SCHOLARSHIP."

"Mum."

"Well, you did."

Looking at me, Jack said, "Not much into fiction."

"You'd fit right in at grad school."

"Like the Westerns, though. Louis L'Amour, ever read him?"

By way of a little bridge-building, I said, "Sure," and really ought to have left it there, but I was prone in those days to nervous logorrhea, and it overtook me now. I knew dick about Louis L'Amour, but started in on how he was an underrated master, a poet of the cowboy code. I quoted Waldo Emerson and Frederick Jackson Turner. Tim was getting sleepy. I gassed on anyway: symbology of the horse, desert mythopoeia. My armpits were swampy. My hairline itched, my whole hot face. When at last I stopped, no one said a thing. I could hear the Duraflame log hissing in its sheath of burn and thought I might barf, or shit my pants, maybe both at once.

Rigid with false aplomb, I fled to the washroom, and cringed on the can. All I produced was a fetid fart. This undigested mess in me. I needed Tums or Rolaids, maybe an Alka-Seltzer, and quietly ransacked drawers. In the last one I tried, to the left of the sink, a bottle of prescription pills rolled from the back and clicked against the hairdryer, its label facing up.

I had seen the word *Prozac* only once, on the cover of *Time* or *Newsweek*, and if someone said *depression*, I still thought first of Roosevelt, but knew what people meant. Apparently, Janice had it. The prescription was for her.

I picked up the bottle and rattled it and peered through its side. Then I popped the safety cap and shook a blue-green capsule into my clammy palm.

When I rejoined the others in the sitting room, conversation carried on as though I hadn't made an ass of myself, and the pill progressed abrasively down my cloggy throat.

⌐

The VCR read 9:08. Janice had opened the windows wide, and was making her second lap of the house, holding aloft a spuming can of potpourri-scented Glade. Tim rinsed mugs and dishes. I stood in front of the fireplace and stared at the dwindled Duraflame log, pretending not to listen to either of my nieces, who were having a giddy go at me, mimicking bulbous stares and thin, squeaky breathing.

"Okay, girls," Janice said. "Teeth and PJs, please. Cheer up, little brother."

"Think I'll take a walk."

"You're not gonna call from the airport, are you?"

"No. Just a walk."

"He's going to Brewster's Pub," said Beth.

Tim said, "That's his business. Teeth and PJs now."

For the second time tonight, Beth thumped my leg.

"Thanks," I said. "Much obliged."

She said, "It's an HONOUR."

⌐

In a booth to myself by the big Scotch pine, I forced a double whiskey down. The pub was all but empty. Less than half an hour ago, I could think of nothing else except being here. Now that I was here, I wanted to go back, catch some *L.A. Law* at ten, then bed and Keats's letters. Mum was going to marry Jack, a decrepit man I didn't know. Sometime soon, he would die. Mum would get his money and end up chucking most of it down the gullet of a slot machine. I thought I should feel *broodier*, and I hunched over my whiskey like a man in an Edward Hopper print, but I was my only audience. The five or six other customers all were sitting at the bar, yakking and keeping an eye on the game, Calgary at Vancouver. Al MacInnis wound up and let one of his bullets go: it dinged off the post. I wanted to give a shit, but hockey was another thing fading from my life. Maybe if the game were played on a pond, and the jerseys had no crests, no affiliations. The Total Anonymities. I could cheer for them.

Yellow and orange-bluish light flickered in the garage windows. I stole a look. Tim in his mask and coveralls welded a broken God-knows-what on his latest project, a deep-purple dune buggy. He called it *Plum Crazy*. I thought I might join him for a chat and maybe even a beer or two, but I had tried that in the past, and it had always felt forced, like handshakes at Camp David. Let him do his thing.

Inside the house, Janice had poured a glass of wine and was sitting on the chesterfield. A book lay open in her lap.

I said, "Sorry to bother you."

She dog-eared a page. "Not at all. Come and sit. Glass of wine?"

"Tepid water."

We laughed and shook our heads.

Janice said, "Poor man."

I sat on the floor in front of her. "Mum is fifty-what?"

"Sixty, in July."

"Still looks good."

"She does."

"Good at her job. Accomplished. Why in the world can she not meet—"

"A halfway normal guy? They see what she wants in a second."

Now a pneumatic drill clanked and rattled in the garage. I nodded toward it.

"How are things with you?"

Janice shrugged. "Okay."

"Okay as in better?"

She turned to look at the darkened hall, then drew her knees up, hugging them, and stared into middle distance. "I'm taking this Child Psych course. You know, as an option. And . . ."

"What's his name?"

"My God, is it obvious?"

"Educated guess."

"Tom," she said. "Mature student. Around my age."

"Okay . . ."

"We've been talking."

"*Talking* talking?"

"After class. A coffee."

"Good-looking guy?"

"More than that. I mean, sure. Tall, athletic body. But he's well-travelled, knowledgeable. Been *all* over Africa. And when we talk, I feel . . ."

"Good?"

She looked around the room. "When did life get beige?"

I said, "Leave."

She said, "I can't."

"Why? The girls? They'll survive."

"I've been married eleven years."

"So?"

She said, "You're young, and I'm tired. Finish this glass of wine?"

"I'm good."

"There if you want it. I have to go to bed."

I sat there by myself awhile, then took the awful wine with me to my basement room and drank it sitting up in bed, leafing through a *People*. Next to the clock radio, Keats's letters lay inert. Just two days before, the book had felt so urgent. I simply had to have it, and I walked out of Odyssey Books into rain on Princess Street, buttoning my trench coat, the book and all its promise shoved down the front of my fraying Levi's. Keats, Keats, Keats. He would show me how to live.

⌐

I woke in my clothes at 2:00 a.m. An awl turned inside my head, and I was very thirsty. On the basement stairs, I thought my ear was ringing—it tends to misbehave when I fly—but then I saw the ghostly light in the vestibule and realized I was hearing a television test pattern. A rainbow spectrum of vertical bars glowed on the Sony, and Tim in his tatty sea-green robe lay fetal on the loveseat. His snore sounded like recess in a distant schoolyard. The remote had slid nearly underneath his ribs. When I tried to ease it out, his eyes fluttered open, and he said, "Time is it."

"Late. Go to bed."

He stood like a forward shaking off a hit, scratched his shaggy paunch, and muttered down the hall. I pointed the remote—*change the battery*—then knelt in front of the set. After I had turned it off, I stayed there a little while, tickling my fingertips in the static on the screen, but sharp, heavy edges torqued in my head. I came back from the washroom with a couple Tylenol, and swallowed them at the open fridge with gulps of Minute Maid. *More*, my body said. I poured another glass, took it to the front room, and sat and watched the tree: red and blue and gold and green, three times all together, then slowly, one by one. I looked for a pattern, memorizing sequences, and do not remember falling asleep or even moving to the lounger. When I woke, a lamp was on, and Beth was a foot away from me, taking a sucker from her mouth.

"Why are you out here?"

I blinked at the clock—7:05—and said I was only dozing.

"You were talking to yourself."

"So. Everybody does."

She mimed the tossing of my head. "'Out of the *way*.'"

"I said that?"

"Yes."

"Were you scared?"

"No. Dad does it all the time."

"Are there any Golden Grahams?"

"He ate them all. Mini-Wheats."

I said, "Even better," and held out my arm.

She put the sucker back in her mouth and grabbed my wrist two-handed. Helped pull me up. The room moved like a ship at sea, and my neck was stiff, but Beth said, "*Allons, mon oncle,*" and dragged me into day.

Janice made feeble joe in an automatic drip thing. I dug out her Bodum and spooned in ruthless heapers. One cup purged my constipated plumbing, and the second was pure shazam. I even worked on my thesis, a slouching and becrippled thing on the minor plays of Beckett, but this morning it felt relevant, my singular contribution to the glory that was Literature. When Janice called my name through the basement laundry drop, I looked at the bedside clock, and then I looked again: three hours had elapsed. I whistled on my way upstairs.

"Sis, I am a genius."

She pressed her palm against the phone. "Mum wants to speak with you."

"Tell her I have cancer."

"She'll marry you," said Beth.

Glenny said "Gross" around the ice-cube in her mouth, and Janice passed the phone.

"Hello, Mother dearest."

"You're in a good mood."

"I just wrote eighteen pages."

"Have you eaten lunch?"

"Need of food subsides in the presence of the *duende*."

"What in the world . . ."

"No. I have not eaten lunch."

"Good. Just the two of us? Then I'll show you Trinity."

"What about Jack?"

"He's out in Okotoks, staying with his family."

"You're doing the old not-seeing-each-other-on-the-night-before thing?"

"We are, yes. Tradition. Shall I pop round now?"

"Need to shower first."

"Chop, chop," she said. "I'm famished."

The waitress cleared our salad plates, and Mum lit a cigarette. Through a French inhale she said, "How are things at the house?"

I shrugged. "Okay."

"You and Tim getting along?"

"Found him on the couch last night. After two, telly on."

"It's hard for him, you know. With Janice off improving herself."

"Mum, she's getting a degree."

"I understand that, but someone has to pay the bills."

"Dad kept a roof over my head. That make him a hero?"

Mum looked at the tabletop, and brushed away focaccia crumbs. "Have you seen him recently?"

"Month, month and a half ago. Nana died."

"He take it hard?"

"Flat on his back in bed, out. Thought he'd tupped himself."

The waitress came with our gnocchi. We watched her

work the pepper mill, and when she was gone, Mum said, "Did he go back for the funeral?"

"Didn't have the cash."

"You're joking."

"No."

"Is he not working?"

"Part-time on the ambulance. A little painting here and there."

Mum stared out the window. "Missed his calling, your dad."

"Doctor?"

"No. That was me. Your dad should have been a singer."

"Could have fooled me."

"He was a lovely tenor. Used to sing to you."

We ate in silence for a while, neither of us with relish.

"How are those first few bites tasting?"

We both answered fine and wore forced grins. I ordered another Valpolicella.

"Mum, mind if I ask a medical question? Draw on your expertise."

"All right."

"I keep hearing about Prozac. Antidepressant drug?"

"That's right. Works neurochemically."

"Does it have any side effects?"

"Aspirin has side effects. Why do you want to know?"

"Curious is all. I mean, I have my funks."

"Depression is not a funk, dear." She pushed her gnocchi round a bit, then said, "Has your dad ever seen someone?"

"You mean like a shrink? Doubt he's even thought of it."

Sheepishly, she said, "Did you tell him about the wedding?"

I said yes without hesitation. "In fact, he sends his regards."

"He does?"

"'Tell her I said congratulations. Hope she's very happy.'"

Mum lit up. "He said that?"

"Been meaning to let you know."

In a sober moment, the old man might remember I was out in Calgary, but not the reason why. I had told him I was spending Christmas with my sister, and I didn't mention Mum, an old unspoken rule. Not once had he asked after her in the years since their divorce, never mind wishing her happiness. But in a lifetime of falsehoods, the one I just told Mum did not rank among the worst, and may even have been worthy. I had not seen her *beam* like that since I was eleven, when she took me to the horse track, and we nailed a fat triactor.

Despite the *caffè lungo*, my energy took a nosedive, and I entered Trinity Seniors Lodge grinding recent dental work. Mum had been head nurse here only since the summer, and I was sure she would be seen as the scheming Grimhilde who had cast a spell on hapless Jack. Rarely have I been more wrong. In the TV lounge and games room, the library and atrium, old folks and personal care assistants smiled at the sight of her. Residents who stopped to chat all spoke of her glowingly. "Special lady, your mom." "What a difference round here." I played the proud, admiring son and didn't have to force it. Gladys, Blanche, Maureen, Bill: she knew every name. Mum was on her turf, exuding expertise.

On our way to see the chapel, she pointed down the hall. "Here comes one of my favourites."

A tiny old woman in a white housecoat left the side of her PCA and tottered straight toward us, carrying a bundle in pale pink fleece.

Mum threw open her arms and said, "Hello, my little duck egg."

The woman lay her veiny cheek against Mum's chest, and stared at me intensely.

"Elsie, honey. This is my son."

Her eyes were blue and bloodshot, glassy but also pre-scient. I felt seen-through and wrong, all my moral lesions lit up as if by X-ray, but she took a baby bottle from the pocket of her housecoat, and urged it into my hesitant hand. Mum threw me a quick wink. I bent toward the swaddled doll, and my head recoiled, it was that realistic: a small, scrunched face, and little, gripping hands.

"What's her name?" I said.

Mum answered. "Rosemarie."

I put the plastic nipple in the puckered plastic mouth and waited a couple seconds.

"Do you think that's enough?"

Elsie nodded and stroked my face.

"Bath time," said the PCA.

Elsie leaned into Mum for another cuddle. Then we watched her go. I asked was it Alzheimer's, and Mum said, "Middle stage. Then suddenly she's lucid, and it breaks your heart, the stories."

"How do you mean?" I said.

"Did you not see her arm?"

"No."

"The number tattooed there. I forget which camp, but it's where her daughter died."

In the silence that followed, I felt myself not having the feelings I thought I should. There was a sense of history and my smallness in the midst of it, my luckiness as well. But the truth is, I was tired, and the rug deodorizer, ubiquitous and strong, was getting to my eyes.

"The chapel," said Mum, "is just round here."

Three meagre rows of five folding chairs had been placed either side of the narrow aisle. A rickety lectern did for a pulpit, and weak track lighting glimmered a tall, tinny cross on the wall above the altar, itself no more than a raised platform. An old upright piano stood against the wall, songbook sitting crookedly on its music rack. In this dim, denuded space, more recess than room, my mother was to marry. "You and I will wait," she said, "until the guests are seated and Jack and the priest are ready. Then we come and stand here. The guests will rise, the music starts, then we proceed."

"Trial run?"

"All right."

She hooked her arm through mine, and I liked how it felt.

"Pace okay?"

"Fine, dear."

Reaching the ersatz altar took ten seconds, if that. I unhooked my arm, and would have turned to go, but Mum stayed where she was, staring straight ahead of herself, hands clasped like a choir girl. A private thought or memory played upon her face. To say she looked *holy* might be pushing it, but hopeful, beautiful, dignified, yes. It was enchanting. Then a voice in the hall shouted, "What is going *on*?" Mum rolled her eyes, and laughed. "Look out," she said. "He's on the loose."

A mad, shaggy creature in denim overalls shambled round the corner. He was pulling an oxygen tank in a metal trolley. Clear plastic tubing hissed up his nose. The chubby PCA in pursuit held his missing shoe, a bright red Converse sneaker. He zigged and zagged away from her, sport sock flopping. Seeing Mum and me, he stopped. "Who the fuck is that?"

The out-of-breath PCA said, "Mr. Dingle, let's try and keep our voices down," then looked apologetically at Mum. "Sorry, Viv. Got away on me."

"Need a hand?"

"I think we're okay."

"I want tapioca!"

"First let's get your shoe back on."

He pointed in the chapel. "What is *happening*?"

"Viv is getting married."

He glared at me and then at Mum. "Are you sick? He's a kid!"

"Mr. Dingle," Mum said. "I'm marrying Jack. You remember Jack."

Bewilderment replaced the crazy lustre in his eyes, and he watched as the kneeling PCA put on and tied his shoe. Then she led him up the hall, and Mum said, "Such a shame. He owned three Tim Hortons."

Mum asked could she drop me off at the LRT. Flo and Larry Vandermeer had invited her to their place for Chinese food and cribbage, and she wanted to make the drive northeast before rush hour hit. I told her that was fine with me. In the car lot at Chinook Station, she opened her purse, "Before I forget," and handed me a hardback book, its light blue covers blank. I looked at the spine: George Eliot. *Silas Marner.*

"You're giving this to me?"

"Have you read it?"

"No."

"It was my favourite book in school."

"Sure you want me to have it?"

"Tell me what you think. Here comes your train."

"Front foyer tomorrow, four o'clock?"

"Three I said!"

"Just joking, Mum."

"Heavens. Give me a heart attack."

"I'll be on time. Have fun tonight."

"Thank you, dear."

I ran and caught the train and sat toward the back of the car, away from a rowdy group of teens. *Silas Marner.* These days, apart from my recent peek into Keats, I read almost nothing except bleak modern plays and involuted theory. Eliot I had read last in my sophomore year. *The Mill on the Floss.* I remembered liking it, very much in fact, and opened *Silas Marner* now, releasing its smell of smoke and time. *Vivian Willets, Lower Sixth* was written in blue on the title page. Never before had Mum shared a thing with me about her past. Now I held a piece of it, and when I read the epigraph, *A child, more than all other gifts / That earth can offer to declining man, / Brings hope with it, and forward-looking thoughts,* I adopted a long and wistful stare, convinced I just had a moment, Cineplex vérité. Climax of

Act Two: mother and estranged son recognize their bond. Cue the cornball music.

Less than an hour later, I was pouring myself another glass of my sister's awful wine, and regaling her and Tim and the girls with tales of Trinity Lodge. I made Elsie's doll even more macabre, and Mr. Dingle zanier. I said the hallways reeked of age, and described the hanging, floppy necks, the bent backs, and the Polident grins. "My *mother*," I said, "the woman who carried me in her *womb*, is marrying in this *charnel house*." Janice and Tim and the girls laughed themselves silly. It was like my schoolboy days, when I did impromptu stand-up for my buddies in the playground: Stop, they said. You're killing me. I swear, I'll piss my pants.

Mum tightened my Windsor knot and showed me to the Xerox room. The two of us were to wait in here before the ceremony. When everyone had been seated and Jack and the priest were ready, Flo would pop in and give us the nod. Mum related all of this in the slow and eerie cadence of someone entering deep shock. I wondered had she popped a tranquilizer, and assured her it would all go well. Off she went to get changed in some other room somewhere, leaving me with a lot of time to kill.

I wandered round the lodge. It was abuzz with wedding talk. Residents stopped to chat with me and compliment my suit. Others admired the chapel, which had been done up in bunting and shimmery white chair covers. Oldsters stood at the dining hall windows and watched as staff in hair nets folded linen napkins. A few fussed as to how and where they would get their supper, but a manager was on hand to let them know they could have it delivered to their rooms or eat in the fireside lounge.

By 3:45, I was back in the Xerox room. Opposite the copier, a big drawer and shelving unit was chock a block with office supplies, including the corrector ribbon for my kind of typewriter. I helped myself to one of those and had just finished pocketing three Bic pens and some Post-it Notes when the door opened, and Mum came in. I said, "*Wow*." Her angled hat was diamond shaped and had a wide-mesh veil attached. Varying depths of burgundy shimmered in her knee-length dress. "Smashing, Mum. Really." Her bouquet was of white roses, and she gave me a matching boutonniere. "Haven't worn one of these," I said, "since my high school prom."

She watched my clumsy handling of the pin and stem. "Here," she said, "let me," but her hands were shaking.

Flo poked her head in. She had the same big ginger hair. "Hey, stretch. Remember me?"

"How could I forget?"

"Doesn't your ma look beautiful?"

"She does indeed."

"Flo, dear. Could you pin this on? My hands . . ."

"No biggie, Viv."

Short and round with big cone boobs, Flo bustled in. "Hold still," she said. The pattern of her low-cut dress recalled *Day of the Triffids*. "There, that oughta hold." She whapped my chest and turned to Mum, whose teeth had started chattering. "Come on now, Viv. You'll be fine. Look at me. You'll be fine."

Mum nodded. "Thanks, Flo."

"Gimme a minute to get sat. Then we're on, okay? Keep her upright, stretch."

"I'll do my best, Flo."

She left the door ajar. I looked at Mum. "Breathe."

"I ought to have the hang of this."

"Tell me when you're ready."

She hooked her arm in mine, stood tall like lessons in poise, and inhaled deeply through her nose.

"All right, dear."

"Sure?"

"Now or never."

"Here we go."

A rheumatic paparazzi waiting in the hall pointed aim-and-shoots, and kitchen staff watched through the dining hall windows. Another throng of old folks had gathered by the chapel. More cameras flashed. I wore a winning grin and winked, and I had a look at Mum. Her face had frozen in a mask of catatonic glee. If I had noticed a moment earlier, then I would have paused and said, Are you all right? but we had turned the corner, and were smack in the chapel entranceway. Standing at the lectern, a dumpy little priest in white and purple vestments wearily regarded us over reading specs. Jack stood to his left, a navy blue suit hanging off the bony pegs of him, and a badly humpbacked old woman dozed at the piano. The priest cleared his throat, then he rustled over and bent toward an ear. With a convulsive start, the woman woke and pounded out "Here Comes the Bride."

Mum and I proceeded past sadly empty chairs. There were a dozen guests in all, six each side of the aisle. Janice and Tim and the girls sat up front on my left. Behind them, Flo elbowed Larry, who quickly slipped his toothpick out, and hid it in his fist. A big bald man on Jack's side squatted in the aisle, and focused his Pentax camera. *Bap* went the flash, blinding me. The next thing I saw was a spider web, black. It spanned the entire shoulderblade of a pale, mangy woman in the second row on Jack's side. The scrawny guy beside her had a mullet halfway down his back. His shoes were Nike high-tops, and he wore a gold cross and chain on the outside of his shirt, with a skinny leather tie. He smiled up at Mum and me, revealing a gold cuspid.

Across the aisle, Glenny caught my eye and pointed deftly at the pianist, who kept on a-pounding as Mum and I passed the two front rows. Twin boys on Jack's side had stuck their fingers in their ears. Baldy with the Pentax threw them an Old Testament look. The hockey-mom-type beside him (heavy rouge, blond highlights) was staring daggers at *me*, as though all this were my idea. I replied with a *Fuck you* look, then delivered Mum to her place beside Jack. His eyes already brimmed. His nose already ran.

Cautiously, the priest went and stood at this end of the Sturm und Drang piano. Only mildly startled now, the woman flubbed a few notes, but threw in a lovely flourish, then up came her hands. Silence had taken a drubbing, but dragged itself back up, and widened in the room.

The priest resumed his place at the measly lectern. Stubble darkened his ruddy jowls, and his purple stole had stains, as though he had wiped his mouth with it, after a greasy beef-dip. The fist he raised to his face failed to mask a sideways jutting of his lips. Gas—*pfft*—parted them. I took my seat, and he began. "Dear friends . . ." His low and ragged voice sounded like a loss of faith. Maybe it was just a cold. I think the cunt had had a few.

In any case, throughout his rote delivery, Mum maintained her trance-like stare. Surely she had noticed and decided to ignore what was happening to Jack: he wept, and as he wept, his snoot issued thick snot. In slow, slithering increments and sudden, startling drops, a matching pair of danglers grew ever longer and slightly pendulous. The priest blethered on. I glanced at Janice—she looked *ill*—and ought to have stood and stopped this farce. The strings of snot were shoelace long. But I didn't do anything, and neither did anyone else. Asked if there were impediments to this holy union, we all kept our traps shut, and the priest moved on to vows (at last). Jack pronounced his hoarse "I will," then caught the swaying length in his cupped and scooping hand. Mum placed the quickest, most tight-lipped of kisses on his wet mustache, and the listing, C-shaped pianist let out a little snore.

Mingling with Jack's family was too hideous a prospect. "Be right back," is all I said, and without even stopping to throw on my coat, blasted right the fuck out the front doors, into the Arctic cold. Aimlessly, I walked the grounds, wincing whenever my head replayed moments of the wedding. Jesus H. What a joke. All of life revealed itself as prolonged mockery! Swearing at the savage wind, I imagined other families, groupings of good and handsome folk gathered at this moment round a Steinway baby grand, sipping mugs of buttered rum, and singing "Good King Wenceslas," or discussing the new biography of Ludwig Wittgenstein—in a house in the country in Vermont, wearing lovely sweaters.

A shovelled walkway on my left meandered into shadow, and something led me up it. Scattered bits of Safe-T-Salt crunched beneath my feet. I came to a small courtyard. A young maple tree hung with silver bells and stars stood in the middle. On its right, a wooden footbridge crossed what would have been in summertime a narrow, winding stream, now a declivity in the snow that lay in neat, even loaves on the seats of benches and nearly buried the garden gnomes. Retching up its ugly song, a magpie perched in the maple tree, and snow glimmered down from the wobbled branch. I rubbed my hands and blew on them and covered my smarting ears. Behind me, a man said, "Brutal, eh?" It was him from the second row, the one with the major mullet. He had put on an open hunting coat over his ill-fitting tan suit.

"Smoke?" he said.

"No thanks."

"Mind?"

"Go ahead."

"You're Viv's son?"

I hesitated, "Yeah."

"Randy. Jack's my dad."

We shook hands. He lit his smoke, and exhaled a mighty plume.

"Like this spot?"

"First time," I said.

"Dad and I used to smoke out here when I came to visit."

He offered me a flask. I had a timid sip. "Rye?"

"Wiser's, Special Blend. Go on, get her in you."

I had an honest haul, and liked its amber burn.

"That's the way, amigo."

I handed it back to him, and he drank off a good two shots. Dragged a wrist across his mouth.

"That was some fuckin wedding."

"Yeah."

"My old man." He shook his head. "Snot was down to here!" He saw my face. "Come on. May as well laugh about it."

I said, "He's your dad."

"He's old, and he knows it."

Shivers ran the length of me. I said, "Well, I'm sorry."

Randy said, "Why?"

"My mom."

"She makes him happy, man."

"Sure about that?"

"Fuckin rights. Shoulda seen Dad a year ago. Could hardly stand. Gave *up* on life. Then he met your mom."

"You say so."

"I *know* so."

A female voice called, "Randy-bear?"

"Up here, babe-a-loo."

Wearing a puffy ski coat, the woman with the web tattoo walked awkwardly in her high heels. "Knew I'd find you here," she said.

"Shootin the shit with Viv's son."

"Hi," she said. "I'm Trix."

"My fiancée," Randy beamed, throwing his arm around her.

"Your mom looked so beautiful. Didn't she Randy-bear?"

"Old man wishes he was younger."

Trix slapped his shoulder. "Pay no attention to him."

"It's okay," I said.

"Aren't you cold? You look cold."

Waggling his flask, Randy said, "Stayin plenty warm."

"Well, Connie wants you back inside. Now, she said. For pictures."

"Is she the one with the twins?" I said.

"That's her all right," said Trix.

"I think she wants to murder me."

Randy said, "Don't worry. Bark's worse than her bite. Get a glass of wine in her, she'll be just fine." He gave his smoke to Trix. "Finish 'er off, snooks."

She took two quick drags and said, "Let's go in. I'm freezing."

"Comin, amigo?"

"You guys go. I need another minute."

"You'll *die* out here," Trix said. "Randy, give him your coat."

He began to take it off.

"I'm fine," I said. "Don't worry. I'll be just a minute."

I watched the two of them, arm in arm, disappear down the walkway. Apart from a swish of traffic out on Elbow Drive, it was very quiet. A big lopsided orange moon hung low in the blue-black sky. I waited for a summative thought, something epiphanic, but mainly I was cold and more or less okay with the silence of my mind.

Turning to go, I saw an old woman watching me from between her partly drawn drapes, from her second storey room. She had on a white housecoat, and I want to say it was Elsie, but that would be untrue. Anyway, I waved at her then beat it back inside, where Mum bustled over and warmed my face in her two hands. "My son," she said. "My beautiful boy. I was so worried. I thought you had gone."

MACINNEY'S STRONG

―――――――――

|

Modern Scottish Poetry. I had ripped it off. The remainder bin at Coles. Maybe half the poems I could actually read. The rest were either in Scots or the Glasgow pidgin—*dizny day gonabootlika hawf shut knife*—that sounded to me like a busted mouth. Staring at the inside cover, I wondered what I would write there—something about heritage, something pertaining to voice—and then as the bus clunked and shuddered into lower gear, I dropped the heavy book in the knapsack at my feet, and stood in the aisle to throw on my coat.

Innisdale had sprawled some. A new marina. Prefab homes. A nativity dripped in one wet yard. Snow had been dusting Kingston when I left at noon, but down here the day belonged to March or early April. Drizzle and grit. Sky the grey of pickerel scales. Up on our left the slow-moving river and its scrawny islands came into view, and the bus swung in at the old hotel. I caught my balance. The old man was there.

When painting had been his trade—his trade and not his fallback—my father had worked in laundered whites and held a soldier's carriage. Now, in a pale green canvas coat, he slouched, and his old grey sweats, torn at the knee, were a motley of eggshell spatters and emerald smudges, chestnut smears and lilac splotches. He didn't see me wave. Fists in the pockets of the pale green coat, mouth working a cough drop or a candy, he was staring up Highway 7 as though the bus were still in the distance. In the window of the hotel lounge behind him a neon *OPEN* fizzled, and I had not slung my knapsack before I could feel the familiar palsy, the living rigor mortis, begin to claim my back and my neck.

Down the steps of the idling bus I followed the paunchy knock-kneed driver, drawing back my shoulders and drawing in the diesel-tainted air before I said, "Dad."

Beneath his dull eyes the wrinkled skin sagged even more than I remembered, but his stride was sure, and his grip still cracked my knuckles.

"Scholar's beard, is it?"

"Wouldn't say that."

"Had to look twice."

I only shrugged and then followed his gaze to the bus driver, who was opening a baggage bay.

"Hey there, chief."

"Afternoon."

"Needin a hand?"

"Got it, thanks."

As the driver hefted an armload of parcels (some in plain brown paper and others in holiday reds and greens), I asked my father where he had parked. He jerked his thumb and said, "Up the road."

I started walking.

He said, "No suitcase?"

I turned on a heel and said, "Told you, remember?"

"Ah, right."

"Have to get back."

He tapped his temple, "Yeah, I remember," and jogged to catch up.

There was a new Subway where Mac's Milk had been, and as we passed that and the small joyful shopfronts, my father whistled a marching tune. On his breath was licorice and mint. A lozenge then. In years past, he had used the same kind up at the rink or when we fished early mornings. Five of the things—glossy black pellets—could fit in the palm of your hand, but in your mouth they were vaporous bombs. I remembered the small tin box they came in, and the name, written in a yellow-green cursive, was coming back to me when my father said, "Heads up, son, this is us here."

I looked at it—a stubby rust-red VW van—and then I looked at him.

"What happened to the car?"

"Thought I told you."

I shook my head.

"Made a trade."

"You didn't tell me."

"Anyway. Give us your bag."

I passed it to him. He reefed open the sliding side door, and as he stowed the bag, Varsol wafting around us, I looked at the jumble-and-sprawl of red and green and cream drop sheets, stiffened brushes and thick-rimmed pots, worn sandpaper and splotchy receipts. Toward the back, I spotted the white wooden box, with its stark red cross and stenciled *FIRST AID*, that I had watched him make twenty years before, just as I had watched him use needle and thread to emblazon the shoulders of his sky blue shirts with crests reading *EMCA*. Now I could not look at him, and even a simple question—"Are you still on the ambulance?"—clotted in my throat. Up in Kingston, it was all different. I took karate. I said my piece. Here, I climbed like a convalescent into my side of the van and made room for my feet amidst a slew of unopened mail and Tim Hortons coffee cups.

Struggling now with the crude seat belt, I saw on the floor beside my father's seat the small selected Yeats I had given him two years ago. Hardened droplets of eggshell white pimpled Yeats's youthful face, and the book was bloated as though it had been left in the rain and the sun. Quickly I checked the inside cover. My clumsy inscription—now partially smeared—came in part from Auden's elegy: *Mad Ireland hurt you into poetry*. We were not Irish, the old man and I, we were Donegal Scots. I mean, he was. What was I? An incomplete curriculum. Of Auden and Yeats I had read only bits entombed in fat anthologies. The kind with notes explaining *Breughel* and *gyre*.

Over on his side, my father now struggled with the door—its latch was not releasing—and, closing the almost ruined book, I leaned across and jerked on the handle. He climbed in and settled and gave the van choke. After two or three tries—"Cooperate, you bitch"—the engine banged into clamour and rattle.

In the quivering side mirror I saw some townies spilling from the hotel. It was now the kind of place with pissy draught and strung-out peelers, but I remembered the Sunday smorgasbords. My father in his Black Watch blazer. The mystery of cocktails. Dim light glinting in polished brass and silverware. At the end of the line, where the man in white presided with carving knife and prong over a shank of bleeding meat, my mother always asked for the heel. On her napkin and on the rim of her glass, on the ends of her Dunhill Lights, the rosy imprint of her lips. These days, she was living with her fourth husband (an invalid ex-army captain) out in a Calgary trailer park.

The townies now were ambling past. One of them waved and shouted a greeting at my father. He did not return it. Revved the van hard. Found first. Released the clutch. With tugboat slowness we heaved into traffic.

II

My father watched the road like a foe. Just past the bridge crossing Trent River, a silvery Honda Prelude pulled out to pass, and as it glided by us the clean-cut driver sounded his horn.

"Know him?" I said.

"Played hockey with you."

"Didn't recognize."

"Doherty. Sean."

I remembered loud dressing rooms and the strawlike smell of a farm kid. Floppy red bangs and squeaky Lange skates. Feigning interest, I said, "What's he up to now?"

"Full time on the ambulance."

"Your partner?"

"Was. I'm back down to part-time."

I looked out the window. Watched the ditch.

"See these places?" my father said, pointing here and there at red-brick green-shingled farm houses. "Bein bought up. People from Toronto. 'Summer homes,' they call them. Palaces, more like."

I nodded.

"Should see the insides. Gut the lot. Full renos."

I nodded.

"Anyway. I can go into one of those places, and," he jabbed his finger at an invisible accuser, "it's twenty bucks an hour, boyo."

"Good," I said, and that was all. Here was our turn. My father whacked the blinker. Far ahead, the taillights of the Prelude disappeared around a bend.

On the bus, I had refused the reeking piss-splashed toilet, and now, as we veered right at the fork in the road, my bowels wrung. Around us, forest thickened and evergreens swayed in squall. Again, my innards twisted as the van jounced down my father's rutted lane. Flagstones leading to his bone-white hut wobbled underfoot, so I walked instead on the sodden oak and maple leaves carpeting the lawn. In the back door window there hung a white wooden goose with a smiling yellow bill and beady black eye. Beneath its feet, a pale blue banner read *WELCOME* in grandmotherly white writing. It clacked against the glass as my father stepped forward and shoved the door open.

The kitchen carpet—mustard with a busy black pattern—had always been grimy, but now it had the look of old scraps put down in a playhouse. Over in the sink, unwashed dishes heaped. A kerosene heater with a half pot of water on top stood in the doorway to my father's bedroom, and an opaque plastic tub with a spigot squatted on the kitchen counter.

Two strides took me to the room he called mine. There, I dropped the knapsack. Flicked the light switch. Four or five times I flicked it, then I slouched in the doorway, one hand on the jamb.

"Come and I'll show you," my father said.

I followed him past the useless fridge—cases of empties stacked up its side—and into the living room. On the fold-out table amidst more unopened mail stood this midgety tree, the kind that comes with the lights attached. My father was pointing. A yellow extension cord. It came in at the side door and through the orange-brown shag it ran to the standing lamp and bulky Zenith at the far end of the room.

"Where," I said, "does it come from?"

"Old missus next door."

"She doesn't mind?"

"Doesn't know. Sit yourself down, now, I'll get the heat on."

I said only, "Toilet."

He said, "One or two?"

I looked at him.

From the washroom he returned with a dark brown bucket. I stood at the front door and watched him lope down to the river. How would we eat? The hospital maybe. He dunked the bucket. Some woman's apartment. Her relatives

111

and us. He lifted the bucket in one hand, and, in the other, six glistening tins of Molson Export.

Reaching into the breastpocket of my blazer, I fingered the return bus ticket redeemable in—I checked my watch—less than sixteen hours. Then I held the door open for my father and accepted the sloshing bucket.

"Remember?" he said.

"Yeah," I said, and he followed me through to the kitchen, where he whistled and opened drawers and cupboards while I was in the washroom. Some of the water I saved for my hands. A brand-new bar of Pears transparent soap lay to the left of the taps, and the hand towel, too, was fresh. On the shelf below the dusty mirror, my father's comb and brush and razor, his bottle of British Sterling, had been placed with military precision. I ran a hand through my hair and appraised my beard a moment—it could still surprise me— then retrieved my blazer and my overcoat from the shower curtain rod. The blazer I put back on, the overcoat I tossed on the bed in the room where I would be sleeping. Leaning against the wall was a fake wooden frame I had failed to notice earlier. In the dim light, I looked closer. A copy of my M.A. I was trying to recall my father having one made when—"Son?"—he called to me from the living room.

"Here, Dad."

"What you up to?"

"Be right there."

In the living room my father was kneeling before the heater (the half pot of water still on top) and filling it from a blue plastic keg with a hose-and-bulb like a blood pressure cuff. "Sit yourself down," he said. "I'll just get this lit."

Beer effervesced in two tall glasses (the PetroCan

112

Olympic ones) standing on the coffee table. Between them on a cutting board was a knife and a brick of crumbly white cheddar. I sat on the brown plaid sofa and watched as my father cranked the knob on the heater. A soft *pop* and its central cylinder began to glow orange-red. My father rubbed his rough hands hard and pushed his palms toward the grate. "Feel that, now, will you." Then he sat in the matching chair opposite and nodded at the cheese. "Lovely, that. Six years old." I nodded. Glass held high, he said, "To your health."

Sipping, I watched him over the rim. He gulped and then smacked his lips, but his hand was steady, and he set his glass down.

"So. What's new in Kingston?"

"Plodding on."

"Up to Montreal?"

"Not in two years."

"Habs are falling apart."

"Pretty busy at school."

"What have they got you readin?"

"All of it seems to start with 'post.'"

"What in fuck does that mean?"

"Not sure I know."

"Used to like it."

"School?"

"Readin."

"Still do, sometimes."

We had some cheese—he closed his eyes and savoured it—and then washed it down and returned to talk of hockey. The Montreal Forum would be closing come March, and my father embellished the forgotten glories of Béliveau and the Gumper.

Steam was now rising from the pot on the heater. I nodded at it. My father ran a hand up and down his stubble and said, "Needin a shave."

"We going out?"

He grinned a little.

"Who is she?"

"Nothin like that."

"Where then?"

"You wait and see."

I took off my blazer and moved farther down the couch. The room was becoming almost too warm, but the beer was good, and he stopped at two.

III

Wafting over the kerosene now was the sharp, piney scent of my father's British Sterling. Fresh-faced, he strode into the living room and said, "Right, then, kid. Time we were off." An overcoat hung over his left arm, and he was wearing his Black Watch blazer. In the light of the standing lamp, its Brasso'd buttons glinted, and his buffed brogues shone.

"Looking pretty sharp, Dad."

Feigning baronial airs, he tugged at his lapels and said, "Do crank off that heat, old fish. No point in burning down the place." Before the mini-inferno I knelt and cranked its knob all the way to the left. My father switched off the standing lamp, and I followed his silhouette through the dark of the kitchen. In the bedroom I groped for my coat, and then outside we took slow steps until our eyes adjusted to the night. The sky had cleared and the wind had abated—low

in the west was a young crescent moon—but the tempera-
ture was dropping. In the van, I watched the pluming of our
breath and obliged my father's palpable need to not tell me
where we were going by asking him where we were going.
He said, "Patience, lad," and sat taller in his seat.

We were climbing Airport Hill by now, and the struggling van dropped to forty as my father shifted from fourth
to third. Then as we peaked and began to descend, he geared
back up and stomped on the gas. The van quaked like a
spacecraft commencing re-entry, and clutching the overhead handle I half expected quarter panels and fenders to
tear free and go whirling out in the night. My father was
laughing, and then he braked—braked hard—and flicked on
the blinker. Ahead on the right was an old gas bar and diner.
"She overheating?" I said, but my father didn't answer and
swung into the lot. There was one other car but the diner
and gas bar both were unlit.

My father cut the engine. I looked again at the darkened
ramshackle diner, and then I looked at my father unbuckling
his seat belt.

"Dad."

"What you waitin on?"

"It's closed."

He began whistling and got out of the van. Slowly, I followed. Here was the place where my father and I had come
umpteen times for toasted westerns and a dozen worms on
our way to the lake, but in the big and silent dark it did not
seem to me a place that anyone should enter.

Running diagonally across the old screen door was a
wooden bar that read *Coca-Cola*, and my father rapped on it.
Without waiting, he opened the screen and the door behind

and leaned in and called, "Hello the place!" Motioning to me, he stepped inside. Like a nervous thief, I followed. Down at the end of the coffee bar, light escaped a curtain drawn across the doorway that led to the kitchen. There used to be double doors there, and I remembered their whop and thud as waitresses answered the bing of a bell or came out plate-laden. Now, as my father called once more, a hand drew back the curtain and out stepped a woman in a white ruffled shirt and black bow tie. A big grin spread across her plump face, and my father stepped forward. "There she is. How are you, love?"

"Just fine, thanks. That your son?"

My father nodded.

The woman walked to me—her eyes big and dancing—and took my hand in both of hers. "So nice to meet you."

I looked at my father and then back at her and said "Pleasure" too stiffly.

Not a bit did it faze her. "Come on back," she said, turning and walking toward the lighted doorway. My father gestured after her, and I followed the woman past the empty booths, each with their jukes. At the lighted doorway, she stood to the side.

"I'm sorry," I said, "but I missed your name."

"Darlene, honey. But you call me Dee."

"All right, Dee."

"Now go on in," she said, winking at my father.

I took two uncertain steps and heard the breath escape me as though I'd just been gut-punched.

Bigger bare tables had been pushed against the walls, but beneath the chandelier's dazzle, there was a small one set for two. Its white and lilac linens matched the walls and trim of the room.

I spun on my heels.

In the doorway, Dee and my father were standing face to face, their elbows cupped lightly in one another's palms. Dee still was grinning, but her face had flushed, and her eyes were wet. "No more fretting, now," my father said, rubbing her upper arm. "It looks magic, love. It does."

Dee stepped back from him and snuffled and took a tissue from her pocket. "I just knew that I'd do this."

My father, meanwhile, had turned to me and was gesturing at the room. "What," he said grandly, "do you think of this?"

Think? There in the doorway to a darkened country diner stood a strange woman dabbing her eyes, and surrounding me was a pastel otherworld.

"We're *eating* here?" I said.

My beaming father nodded.

I looked at Dee. "Wasn't this the kitchen?"

"Used to be," she nodded. "We built a new one just through there."

I followed her pointing finger. In the room's far corner, there was a swinging door. A face appeared in its porthole window, and then the door swung inward: a lanky man in white.

"Hey hey," my father said.

"'Ello, my friend!"

He was fiftyish and bald, but wore a heavy blond-grey beard. He shook my father's hand, and then they embraced (I had never seen my father hug another man) before regarding one another like relatives in airports. The man's right eye was droopy, but his left was wide and glinting and focusing on me as he said, "Your boy?" The accent was

117

French, but there was something else. An impediment. An epiglottal thickness.

My father was nodding—proudly, he was nodding—and, excitedly, he said, "Son, this is Gabby."

The man pumped my hand and said, "Welcome, welcome! We 'ear so much about you." Now he was clasping my shoulder as well. "Your father," he said looking down. When he looked at me again, his good eye was wet. Letting go of my hand he said, "I am sorry." Then he stepped back and flung his arms wide and *smack* went his heel on the floor. "*So,* what you think of my little bistro?"

All the lilac seemed to me sickly, but I said, "Looks great."

"Your father, he do a good job."

I nodded.

"Okay! Enough my talking. I see you later." He looked at Dee. "They have the cocktails?"

"Give them a chance to sit down, why don't you."

"But of course, sit!" he said, thrusting his hands at the table. "We get you some drinks, and I make you a meal you're never gonna forget!"

On his way by, the man slapped my shoulder. Dee took our coats and drew back both chairs from the table. Sitting, I noticed a small menu card with calligraphic writing all in French. I had studied French. I had bandied terms like *l'autre* and *il n'y a pas de hors-texte*, but I could not understand or pronounce even in my head most of the words on the menu.

"Now," said Dee, "a cocktail to start, maybe Champagne?"

Quickly, I said, "Just water will do."

"Sparkling?" she said. "Or do you like still?"

"The kind," I said, "that comes from a tap." My father's eyes were on me. I was able to meet them, and I felt both relieved and righteous when he told Dee that he'd wait for the wine.

"I'll bring you a list," she said, clasping my shoulder on her way by.

The swinging door behind me had not completed its motion when my father said, "*Hey*," and toed me just beneath the knee.

"What."

"They're doin this for us."

Rubbing my knee I said, "The local charity cases."

His teeth bared, and I watched the fist begin to ball then relax as behind me the door swung inward. A moment later, Dee appeared. On her tray stood two slim glasses garnished with lemon twists and a gleaming blue bottle of spring water. In her right hand she carried a wine list. This she handed to my father, but he nodded at me as though deferring to connoisseurship. As Dee filled the water glasses, I glanced over a panoply of mostly French wine. Some of the bottles topped a hundred bucks. Good. If my father had painted this place for our supper, then we would drink rich. But when Dee asked me, "See anything you like?" I could only look at her, plebian heat in my face. "Why don't I serve you by the glass?" she said, explaining that a white would go better with our salads, while the main required a red. She ran through some suggestions, and her voice was so bell-like, her manner so authentic—so unlike some five-star snob—that my shame and my petulance melted.

"How long have you had this place?"

She grimaced a little, as though hiding a pain in her hip, and looked at my father. "What is it, now, handsome, almost a year?"

My father nodded.

I said, "Unique combination, diner and fine dining."

"Trying it out for now," she said. "Gabby wants to tart the whole place up."

My father said, "No more flippin burgers."

"I don't mind so much," said Dee. "Whatever pays the bills."

Off she went—giving my shoulder another squeeze—and into the silence between my father and me I said, "Sorry. She seems nice."

"Tip to toe," my father said and took a sip of his water.

"How long have you known them?"

"Since they bought the place. In for a coffee on my way to work. Know how it is. Get to talkin."

I nodded at the menu. "This Gabby's a chef?"

"Yeah," said my father, "trained in Europe."

I lowered my voice. "Was it a stroke?"

"Eh?"

"Gabby," I said, pointing to my eye.

For a moment my father closed both of his, and after opening them again he looked over my shoulder and said, "Not now." Dee had come in.

From a small decanter she poured white wine into our glasses, and then she placed two salads before us. After saying the name in French, she listed the ingredients in English. Amidst the varied greens (one of them looked thistly), there was fennel and shavings of cheese and little orange wedges or maybe pink grapefruit. I don't remember gourmet meals. I remember barbecues. I remember perch fillets. There were Cornish hens that night, I do remember that. Inside them was a mash of herbs and veg and bits of zingy sausage.

On every course, as Dee presented it, and then again as she cleared our plates, my father and I lavished praise. We told her how we could taste the spices, and how the wine went well with them, but when she was out of the room, we masticated mouthfuls and handled our silverware as though encircled by sniggering snobs. What did we know of tannins and thyme? We knew liver. We knew leeks.

I asked my father, "Think this place'll fly?"

"Hope so," he said.

"Where're they from?"

"Dee and Gabby? Montreal."

"How in the world did they end up here?"

My father looked at the carcass of his hen, and, shrugging, he said, "How in the world does anyone?"

Silence 'til dessert. A swan-shaped pastry stuffed with strawberries and cream and floating on a puddle of chocolate and liqueur. Drizzled with strawberry coulis. My father could not finish his. "Go on, lad, get that in you." I got it down to please Dee, who offered coffee and digestifs. I looked at my father, flushing now after his third glass of red, and I said, "Think we've kept these folks long enough, Dad."

It was then that Gabby whumped in the room, holding in his left hand three clinking snifters, and in his right an ornate bottle. To Dee, he said, "A seat," and she said, "I think they're on their way, hon." He gestured in a Gallic way—thrusting lips, a prolonged shrug—and said, "Just a little brandy, no?" Dee said, "I'll get the coffee," and left the room. Gabby sat and poured three fingers in each snifter. "My best," he said, "XO." Apart from "expensive," I neither knew nor cared what XO meant, but once we had raised our glasses and Gabby had said, "*Santé!*" I took a princely sip and nodded as though the burn were delicious and familiar. My father knocked back most of his. Gabby poured him three more fingers and, after setting down the bottle, clapped the tabletop. "*So*, you tell me, how is your meal." I told him it was marvellous and wished him luck with his new venture. Modestly, he shrugged. "At first, I think, no chance this place. But your father he say to me, 'Gabby, you can do it.' Now, I try." They raised their glasses and drank as Dee came in. Her face was flushed, and coffee spilt into the saucers as she served us. Gabby hardly noticed as he said to me, "You are at the university."

I nodded.

"Big scholarship."

I shrugged.

"Gonna be the *professeur*."

"Times I wonder."

"Me, I have a son at the university."

On her way by, Dee said, "McGill."

I watched her go, and then to Gabby I said, "Montreal's a good town."

He grasped my forearm. "You like the Habs."

I nodded.

He touched my glass with his. We drank. "Your father say you are the goalie."

"Was."

Gabby clapped his chest. "Me too." Then he leaned closer and pointed at a pale scar, the ends of which could be seen above and below his bushy eyebrow. "No mask those days." He leaned back. "Your father, he say you were good in the net."

I remembered pucks sliding between my legs or fluttering

past my catcher, and my father in the stands, shaking his head. "I think the old man may be telling tall tales."

Gabby playfully slapped my shoulder and smiled so much at my father that his right eye was no more than a fissure. I swallowed what remained of my brandy and pushed back my chair. Gabby grasped the bottle and said, "You have another."

"No," I said. "No, thank you."

He spread his thumb and forefinger. "Just a little traveller."

My father said, "Gabby."

"*Oui* my friend."

"We should let you and Dee to your Christmas."

Gabby looked from my father to me and then at the tabletop. "Okay. Another time I see you."

"Maybe some time in the spring," I said. "Thanks for all this, really."

His good eye was solemn as he said, "My pleasure."

The three of us stood, and Dee came in with my father's coat and mine. Farewells began. Over Dee's shoulder as she hugged me, I watched my father and Gabby clasp-and-clap like kin again. In my ear, Dee said, "Take care of your dad. He's one special guy." I nodded, and thought of the stolen anthology.

IV

We sat awhile in the idling van. My father was staring out the windshield as he had been staring up Highway 7 when the bus pulled in. Then he shook his head while finding reverse and said only, "Gabby." I thought that he might speak as the van left the parking lot, but once he had geared up, a gloom came over him, and over me too. Our fancy meal was done. His dowdy shack and his stumpy tree and—already in my guts the rich sludge roiled—his brown bucket awaited us.

The van now trundled up Airport Hill, its feeble beams disappearing in darkness a few yards ahead. Ours was the only vehicle on that stretch of Highway 30, and the distance between Dee and Gabby's and my father's turnoff seemed like double or triple. I realized then how much the van had slowed down after descending the hill, and I looked at my father. His vacant stare. Then he said, "Me and Doherty. We took the call."

"What call?"

"Coupla months back. Near ten at night. An accident at Gabby's. Between you and me, this."

I said, "All right."

"We went out Code Three," he said. "Wheeled into the lot. 'Place looks all closed up,' I says, but then we see Dee screamin out the door. Smeared with blood. 'You all right?' I says. She nods, but the face on her. 'Where's Gabby?' I says, and she can hardly say, 'Upstairs.' 'Mind she's all right,' I tell Doherty. Then I get my bag and go in. Just back of the old kitchen I find this rickety flight of stairs. Up I go. Some rooms up there where Dee and Gabby stayed when they first bought the place. Stunk of grease, but she'd done it up nice. Curtains and all. Anyway. 'Gabby!' I says, and I hear this grunt. The bedroom. I thought, What in fuck? So in I go and there's Gabby slumped against the bed. Legs straight out in front of him. His face swollen all to hell, and blood—I mean *soppin*—from here to fuckin here." My father touched his chin and his thigh.

"Conscious?" I said.

"Wide awake. Looks at me and waves hello. I says, 'Gabby, what have you done?' 'Hut-masel,' he says. 'Hurt yourself? Yeah, I see that, Gabby. How?' Doherty's there now and has a look. 'Holy Christ!' he says. 'Shush,' I tell him. 'Gabby!' I says. 'Look at me, now. What have you done?' He shakes his head and says, 'Ah uck'n *hut* masel.' Then he cocks his finger. Points it at his mouth. 'Tellin me you *shot* yourself?' He nods. 'O Christ,' Doherty's moanin, 'O my fuckin God.' '*Quiet* now,' I tell him, and 'With what?' I says to Gabby. He jerks his thumb back over the bed. I step round. There it is."

"The gun?"

"Lyin right there on the floor. He'd been settin on the other side of the bed. Gun in his mouth." My father opened his own mouth wide and for a moment put his finger in it. "Bang! It sent him straight across the bed and down the other side."

"Impossible," I said.

"How do you mean?"

"The gun was in his *mouth*?"

"Angle. Straight back and he'd have blown out his spinal cord, but it was like this." My father poked the roof of his mouth. "Through the hard palate, deflects this way and lodges in the skull, just here." He pushed his cheek in and up against his eye.

"What did you do?"

"Doherty wasn't much help to me, I'll fuckingwell tell you that. Hands on him shakin." My father held out his hand and trembled it. "Anyway. Staunch the blood and in the rig and blast on down to Kingston."

"You drove."

"No. Doherty was better off up front. I stayed with Gabby. Kept him awake."

"How?"

"Jokes and stories."

My father hit the blinker and we said nothing more until we were in his drive, the engine off and neither of us moving in the dark. "Why," I said, the heart in me banging, "have you never told me this before?"

My father shrugged. "Tellin you now."

"He all right these days?"

"Gabby? They're still rebuilding his mouth. Sees a what-do-you-call-it."

"Speech therapist."

"Aye, that too."

I unbuckled my seat belt and so did my father, but as I pulled on the door handle he said, "I asked him, you know."

"Asked him."

"You know who means it. I've picked them up. I've scraped them up. On the wrists it's a full deep X. Right to the fuckin bone." My father emitted a sound between a retch and a snarl. "You could say he should have used a shotgun. Lots of them do. No comin back from that. But I've seen smaller guns than what Gabby used do the job. He fuckingwell meant it, and I asked him. Coupla weeks back, I says, 'You didn't fart round the edge and have a wee peek. You fuckingwell *dove*.' He nods at me. He says, 'Yeah.' I says to him, 'Well then. What's it like down there?'"

Some moments later I asked, "What did he say?"

My father's answer was a slow, simian shaking of his head, but on our way to the cottage he grasped my arm. "Watch your step, son. Those leaves are slippy."

V

While my father carried the standing lamp into his bedroom and closed the door behind him, I stayed in the living room, where the kerosene stove glowed like a tribal fire and warmed a pot of water to wash with before bed. The last two tins of beer were still coldish, and I opened both and filled our glasses. My father came in holding the lamp like a standard in his right hand, and on the left he balanced two gifts in silvery wrapping.

"We said just one, Dad."

"This year's different."

"Give us the lamp?" With it I went through to the kitchen and, checking my shoulder, ducked into his room. There on the bed lay a three-pack of wrapping paper with two of the rolls unused. I tore at the plastic and grabbed one (bells and holly on a red background) and then, amidst the litter of coins and receipts and mismatched cufflinks on his dresser, I saw the Scotch tape and yellow X-Acto.

Calling "Won't be long" on my way across the kitchen, I went into the other room, and there I ineptly wrapped *Modern Scottish Poetry*. Despite the cool air, my armpits were swampy. I took off my blazer and brought both gift and lamp into the living room.

"Nice paper, that."

"I think ahead."

"Hang on, now." My father unplugged the lamp and then plugged in the little tree. It was pretty. He said, "You start."

I said, "All right," and began with the smallest box. A bottle of British Sterling. "Won't have a beard forever," he said.

"Probably not. Thank you, Dad."

"Welcome. On you go."

The next box was large but light, and I thought it held a sweater, but my father was grinning impishly.

It was a Habs home jersey. Not until I held it up did I see the signatures.

"Don't know what to say."

"Let's see it on you."

"Shouldn't wear it."

"Once won't hurt."

I stood and burrowed into the jersey. Pulled it down. Examined unfamiliar names.

"Your man's not there," my father said, referring to Patrick Roy, who had recently been traded to the Colorado Avalanche. Back in Bantam and Midget, I had copied his V-stance. "Missed him by a week or two."

"It's okay. Thank you."

"Welcome."

"Was it Gabby?"

"His son. Knows a guy who does physio for the team."

"I'll pop in and thank him."

"He'd like that. Looks good, doesn't it?"

I struck a V-stance and awkwardly sat down, the tightness returning to my shoulders and neck as I looked at the remaining gift.

"My go, is it?"

"Sorry it's just the one."

"Never you mind." I watched while he popped tape and slid the book free. "Poems!" he said, in two syllables, and then reached across the table to shake my hand hard. "Been needin a new one."

"New one?"

"That Yeats you gave me."

"In the van."

"I've worn it out."

"You liked it?"

"Pick and choose a bit. Faeries and the end of the world, no thanks, but that tread softly, now, for you're treadin on my dreams—know that one?"

"Not very well."

"Fuckin great. Makes a difference."

"How do you mean?"

"Rhythm of my day. The guys in that ambulance office. Parked in front of the goggle box. Game shows and soap operas. Grown fuckin men? Give your head a shake. I take a walkie-talkie and go on up the stairs. Quiet place near the tuck shop."

"I remember it."

"Tea and read. Same when I'm paintin."

I nodded at *Modern Scottish Poetry* and said, "Don't want to lug that one around."

"Aye, hefty."

"It has lots," I told him, "that other ones leave out." But I'm not sure he heard me. He was leafing pages. Here and there he paused and his gaze concentrated. Other times, his face relaxed wholly. Then he laughed to himself and said, "Like that one."

"Read it."

"Out loud?"

"Out loud."

His shoulders came up, but he said, "All right," and swallowed some beer. Then he cleared his throat, and in the accent that was his when I was a boy he read,

helluva hard tay read theez init
stull
if yi canny unnirston thim jiss clear aff then
gawn
get tay fuck ootma road

ahmaz goodiz thi lota yiz so ah um
ah no whit ahm dayn
tellnyi
jiss try enny a yir fly patir wi me
stick thi bootnyi good style
so ah wull

"You read it great, Dad."

"Think so?"

"Yeah."

"Lemme find another."

I nodded but stifled a yawn and said, "Sorry."

"Fadin?"

"Guess so. You?"

"Think I'll sit a wee while. If that water's too hot, you can cool it some from the jug out in the kitchen."

"What about the lamp?"

"I'm fine sittin here."

I tested the water with my fingertips—it was hot but not scalding—and took the pot in one hand and the lamp in the other, leaving my father by the now unlighted tree. The lamp I stood just outside the washroom door, and then I plugged the drain and poured half of the steaming water into the sink. Over the shower curtain rod, I carefully draped the autographed jersey. Two player names, Vincent Damphousse and Mark Recchi, came back to me, and I was searching for their signatures when my father called, "Just out for a pee!" "Okay!" I answered, lathering my face and neck with Pears. The hot water was a magnificence, and, standing, I let it trickle down my back and my chest. Then I listened. I listened hard. Called my father. Called him again.

Snatching the lamp, I ran to the front. Bashed the door open and the screen. It smacked hard against the outside of the cottage, and down at the river my father whipped round.

"Fuckin hell, boy. Threw a fright in me."

"What are you doing?"

He pointed up. "Lookin at stars."

"Coming in?"

"Minute. Get that door shut. You'll let out the heat."

I ran back and threw on the jersey and then joined my father. He pointed east. "Orion," he said. Then, pointing north, "There's your Big Dipper, Ursa Major too."

Shivering and goosefleshed I said, "Beautiful."

"Some nights," he said, sweeping his arm across the sky, "it's a fuckin *blizzard* of them, son, and diamonds in the river."

After a silence, and tensing my body against deep shivers, I said, "Dad, the PUC bill."

He said, "What about it?"

I said, "How much?"

He looked down. "A thousand. Plus the same again."

"Same again?"

"Reconnection charge."

"I can give them that."

My father shook his head.

"Scholarship cheque. Comes next week."

"Keep your money, son. You deserve it."

"Dad, it's a fuckin joke what I do." What did I do? I went to bed late. I got up late. I ate pho. I worked out. For this, the Social Sciences and Humanities Research Council of Canada was giving me three times what I'd lived on as an undergraduate, and here was my father in Scottish coal mines by the age of eighteen, and in the British army by the age of twenty-one. "Dad," I said, "let me loan it you at least."

"Coupla jobs comin up. Big one on Grand Road. Umpteen rooms. I'll be all right." Calmly, my father reached in the left pocket of his blazer, and a moment later I heard the tinny rattle as he took out the box and shook a lozenge into his palm.

"What are those called again?"

"MacInney's Strong. 'For Your *Best* Voice.' Want one?"

"Please."

As the lozenge began its aromatic work, I looked upriver to the pair of islands in the middle of the channel, and I remembered shivering in the prow of an aluminum ten footer my father had long since sold. I was eight years old then, and collared in a lifejacket. My father, newly full time on the ambulance, had bought me my own rod. On the obsidian early-morning water, my bobber hardly moved. Down in the stern, my father sat facing the opposite direction, and I watched the spangle of his vaulting lure and the motion of his forearm as he jigged. Between us lay the new first aid kit and his pale green tackle box. On the top tier with the leads and sinkers I saw the MacInney's Strong. Quietly, I reeled in and gently stowed my rod, and then down the boat I stole. Got hold of the tin. Eased up its lid. Between my thumb and first two fingers I pinched four and then five of the glossy black pellets and in one go I popped them. Made as

132

much spit as I could. Scour and scorch in my nose and throat, but I swished the lozenges and then locked them beneath my stupefied tongue. I knew what my father could do. I knew about his breath. It could stopper the mouths of the dying and keep their souls inside their bodies, and I hoped that I might pilfer just a portion of that magic.

TWO

TWO

LURE

On their way down to Ecky's for an oil change and filters, his father pulls into Canadian Tire. Stares at lures as long as his hand. Shimmering eyes and thick as sausage—the long wicked dangle of treble-barbed hooks—they look like specimens bungled by God. Or something older than God. And crueller.

As his father slides a box—called Heddon's Cobra—from a prong, the boy slips round the end of the shelf. Walks past the spinners and the hairy buzzbaits to the display of shiny spoons. Sees the Red Devil. Notes the price. Moves down the aisle. Stands on tiptoes—his father is reading the back of the box—then scans the display of rods and sees the one his father got him. Checks the tag. Then the selection of open-faced reels. Finds one like his then does the sum. Knows they are not poor. But knows they don't have heaps. He feels the weight of forty dollars.

His father says, Son?

The boy scoots back and says, I'm here.

Suppose we should be going.

Gonna get that one?

Thought I might.

Maybe it's the charm.

Over the box, his father makes a jokey cross. Hope so, he says.

They walk to the cash, and his father pays half with Canadian Tire money and half with real. Then they drive to Ecky's. Pull up in front of the service bay. A car in there with its hood way up. The boy's father rolls down his window. Leans his head out and makes a bullhorn with his hand. Weren't you fixing that one last week?

Ecky leans around the hood and says, You're next.

Only kidding, Hector. Take your time.

His father turns off the car. Shall we pop up to Wing's?

The boy says, Sure.

They get out and his father tosses the keys in the car. They bounce beside the bag with the lure in it.

Up at Wing's, they sit at the counter, and his father nods hello at the men always there. The waitress named Mary is down near the end talking to a guy in a Rough Riders coat. She puts down her smoke and says, Hey, Morris. Tea?

The boy's father says, Coffee, I think.

And then Mary looks at the boy. He looks at his father.

Tell her what you'd like, lad.

The boy looks back at Mary. Root beer?

Fountain or can.

The boy says, Can. And then he says, Please.

Mary serves them and says, How's Carol?

And the boy's father says, She's well.

Good to hear, says Mary, and she looks down the counter.

The boy's father says, Back on the fags?

Hard when you work in a place like this.

Hard anytime.

Want a menu, Morris?

Fine just now.

Back in the kitchen, Wing hits the bell and says, Pick up pick up. Mary goes. The boy bends his straw and watches his father pour cream in his coffee and stir long and slow as he looks down the counter and joins in the blather—jokes, the weather, Trudeau, and who's died. The boy drinks his Hires. Turns on the stool. But only a little. Nibbles his straw. Closes one eye and looks in the can. His father turns back. You peckish?

The boy looks up. French fries?

His father nods. Orders a plate and they share. With malt vinegar.

Not bad these.

Mum's are better.

So I'll have the last one.

The boy looks at it. His father says, Yours, and he slides two bucks under the plate. They get up to go. Wing comes out for a swallow of Coke. Wipes his shiny forehead with the length of his arm and says, Hello, Morris, how are you how are you?

Good, Wing. Yourself?

Oh, busy busy. Plan for weekend?

Fishing, Wing.

This time of year? Weather no good.

Perfect for muskie.

A couple of men at the counter look over and Wing stops drinking his Coke. Looks at the boy and says, You go?

The boy only nods.

And Wing says, Wow. Then he spreads his arms wide and says, Big fish.

The boy nods again.

And Wing says, Be careful he no eat you.

The men at the counter laugh, and the boy looks at Mary. She blows out smoke and smiles at him. The boy looks down. His father waves bye to her and to Wing, and Wing says, Bye! Good luck good luck!

A man at the counter says, He'll need it he'll need it. And laughs with the others as the bells on the door—three of them on a shiny red ribbon—bounce and clang and rattle behind the boy and his dad.

Up at Ecky's the car isn't done. The boy and his father stand in the bay. Grease stains and tools. Sunshine Girls all over a wall. And on the wall opposite a huge stuffed muskie—Ecky says *lunge*—on a fancy piece of wood with a brass plaque. The boy's father has another look and shakes his head. Forty-eight pounds, Hector.

Under the car, Ecky says, Yep.

Must have been a fight.

Ecky slides out and looks at the fish but doesn't say anything. Slides under again.

The boy's father says, What did you use?

Ecky says, Eh?

His father says, Bait.

And Ecky says, Frog.

The boy's father crouches and looks under the car. Plastic? he says.

Nope, says Ecky. Real.

Can't say I've tried it.

Hardly use anything else. For muskie.

Never jerkbait?

Ecky slides out and stands up. You know why they call it that?

I think I hear what you're saying, Hector.

Ecky wipes his hands on a rag. Don't mind my sayin—

Go ahead.

Saw that eight-dollar gizmo on the front seat.

The boy says, Really it was four.

Yeah, well. You're goin up to Crowe, right?

The boy and his father nod.

Lotta shoals out there, Morris. Weedbeds—right between the islands there—perfect.

The boy's father nods. That's where I trawl.

Had a follower?

Earlier this fall. I could *see* it, Ecky. Not ten feet from me. It *nudged* the lure. Like it knew, the bugger.

It won't nudge a frog.

How does one—

'Tween the islands there. The ones closer to the western shore. Lob it out on the lily pads. Let it sink a little. Jig it a bit. Don't reel too fast.

What sort of hook?

Big one, laughs Ecky. And he hooks his finger—his filthy, pointed nail—beneath the boy's chin. Put it through here, he says. Then he turns out his leg like a Sunshine Girl. Or here. Points near his crotch and says, The meaty part. It'll kick. Bleed a little. Hello, fishy—he nods and smiles—that's what you want.

Where will I find live frogs this time of year?

Place outside of Marmora. I know the guy. When you goin.

Tomorrow, first thing.

I'll call him.

Thank you, Hector.

No bother.

The boy's father turns around and looks at the muskie again. So does the boy. The snout on it. The teeth. The boy's father says, One hell of a fight.

And Ecky says, Why it's on the wall, Morris.

Can one man land it?

Ecky points at the boy. He goin with you?

His father's hand on the boy's shoulder. Yes, he is.

Ecky horks in a grease stain—it jiggles and glistens—and looks at the boy. Guess, he says, you get to gaff the whore.

At home, as they pack the car, the boy's father hefts the big polehook and says, Like this, son. Through the gills. Then you lift it in the boat, and, if it's still fighting, I'll bash it with the truncheon. Try.

The boy takes the hook. Looks at the horrible barb. Tries to picture the fish. Grips the pole hard. Behind him, his mother opens the door to the kitchen. The boy swings the hook.

142

Morris, says his mother, what on earth is he doing with that?

He's fine.

Dad, I don't think I'm strong enough.

Son, with my luck, you won't need to be.

The boy looks at his mother. She shakes her head and says, Supper.

The boy and his father quickly wash up and then sit down in the kitchen. It's mostly leftovers. His mother says she'll make sandwiches with the rest of the roast and wrap up the last of the cake as well. Then she goes to her room while the boy and his father wash the dishes. After that, they finish packing the station wagon, and the boy watches as his father hitches the trailer and backs out to the end of the drive so there won't be so much noise in the morning. They go back in and his father says, Make an early night of it. The boy walks down the hall, but the washroom door is closed, and he can hear his mother having a bath. He walks back to the living room, but his father is not there, and then the boy hears the scraping of the chair on the floor in the basement and knows his dad will be there awhile. Sharpening hooks. Or doing maths. Or just sitting there.

In his room, the boy sets his alarm just in case his dad sleeps in. Then he gets on the bed and kneels at its edge. Imagines the gaff in his hands and *swings* it. Then lies back. Stares at the ceiling. It has a new crack.

The release of the lock on the bathroom door. His mother's footfalls. He reaches over his nightstand and opens the door a little. She still knocks. He says, Come in. She smells of steam and coconuts. A towel on her head the way women twist it. The boy sits up. His back against the headboard.

She sits on the edge of the bed. Looks around his room a moment. He says, All done in the washroom? She nods. He says, Have to get ready for bed.

All right, says his mother. Just came in to say—hope you have fun.

We will.

You don't have to do anything you don't want.

The boy looks at his feet and says, The presents said from both of you.

His mother says nothing. Then touches his knee. And she says, Wear your life jacket. Starts to stand.

But the boy says, Promise.

And she leans toward him. Her bathrobe bulging at the top. The boy can see down it to the diagonal slash of scar but looks away, and they hug hard.

It was good on my birthday, Mum.

She stands and sniffs. I'd best make your sandwiches.

In the bathroom, the boy swipes the mirror and does behind his ears. Then his teeth and a gargle and he splashes the sink clean. Gives the taps and faucet a shine with the facetowel.

On the way back to his room, he sees his mum standing at the counter with bread and wax paper and the rest of the beef. She's holding a knife that has butter on the end, and she's looking out the window. And humming.

In his room, he lies down and puts his hands behind his head. Hears his mother finish up in the kitchen and go to her room. Listens for his father coming up the basement stairs. Then lets his eyes close.

When they open again, it is dark and his arms are numb. He slips them out from beneath his head and flops them down one at a time, and they go pins and needles as he rolls over and squints at the clock—a quarter to one. Hum of the fridge. The heat coming on. Moon on his pillow. He turns the clockface away. Breathes out his nose. Falls back asleep but keeps seeing the frog. As though from beneath. Up through the murk where it kicks and kicks in the warm and the light. He rolls over again and hears the pulse in his ear then opens his eyes and gets out of bed. Kneels at the foot. Head on his fists. And his lips move, but he's not really talking. Doesn't know what to ask. Then he sits on his hands at the edge of the bed. Looks at the moon. Then closes his eyes and tries to think nothing until he hears his father trying not to make noise in the kitchen. Running water. Kettle on. The *k-tunk* of the lid on the tea canister. Three heapers of sugar in the tall orange Thermos. The kettle unplugged before it starts whistling. Water poured into the Thermos and the lid screwed on before his father gives it a shake. Footsteps in the hallway. 5:01. A knock on the door with just one knuckle, and then he pushes it open and takes a step in and stops short when he sees the boy standing.

I'm ready.

Shhh.

The boy nods and follows his father to the darkness of the kitchen, where they share a glass of apple juice and lean against the counter. His father hands the boy the glass and nods at what's left. The boy gulps it down. Puts the glass beside the sink and looks at the new pink J-cloth draped over the faucet. His father unscrews the Thermos cap and lifts out the tea bags—four of them—by their corners, like the tails of small steaming fish. Drops them in the sink—it still smells of Ajax—and screws the lid and the cup back on and reaches for

145

the cooler on the counter. But the boy says, I've got it. And follows his father like a thief through the hush of the house. By the door, they step into shoes, and his father nods at the boy's windbreaker hanging from the middle hook. He opens the door. Birds. Moon. And crickets.

The boy puts on his windbreaker and shivers on his way to the wet-gleaming car. The engine idles smoothly, and the boy's father says, Well done, Hector. And the boy remembers the fingernail. The little notch it made.

As his father reverses, the boy looks at the blinds on his mother's bedroom window. Thinks he sees a chink. Waves a little. His father doesn't notice. Doesn't speak. Just drives. North. Highway 28. Then east on 7. The car very warm. The boy's eyelids heavy. His head bobs. He resists. Then doesn't. Feels between his ribs some time later the thumb of his father. Opens his eyes. Sky the same colour as a splayed lake salmon. But the boy says, Beautiful. He blinks hard and gives his head a shake. Looks around. They have left the places that feel like places. Here is like pictures in Art and Geography. Granite. An esker. Jackpines. A river.

Much farther?

His father says no. Turns on the radio then hits the middle button and twists the knob a bit. Mostly cloudy, a high of six, chance of showers in the late afternoon, some gusting. His father says, Good. Then turns down the volume. People talk about the hostages in Iran and then the boy sees a homemade sign—*LIVE BAIT 1 M*—on a telephone pole. He looks at his father. Looks up ahead. Sees a small shop and says, Looks closed.

Could be, says his father. We'll just have to see.

They pull in. Tall weeds and a camper beside the ramshackle

146

shop. His father turns off the car and gets out. A cat the colour of butterscotch candy—and with only three legs—comes round the corner of the camper. And then the camper's door swings open and smacks the camper's wall, and a man with messy hair and his shirt untucked steps out and zips his jeans up. Looks at the car and at the boy's father. Nods when the boy's father says something and walks to the shop. The boy's father follows. So does the cat. A hand—a woman's hand—and arm in the camper's doorway. Groping for the door. Pulling it shut. At the door to the shop, the man takes keys out of his pocket and shoves the cat with his foot. Opens the door and turns on a light, and before the boy's father closes the door behind him, the cat scoots in, and the boy sees on the wall at the back of the shop a display of tackle and above it the stuffed head of a buck and its fortress of antlers. Then the door opens a bit, and the man leans out and tosses the cat. It lands okay then turns around and watches the door.

The boy shifts. Adjusts the rear-view. Looks at his eyes and then at the rods and the net in the back of the car. The truncheon. And the gaff. He readjusts the mirror then rubs his eyes and looks at his hairless forearms. His spindly hands and broomstick wrists.

The door of the baitshop opens, and his father—facing in the shop—nods goodbye and turns around and walks to the car with a white plastic pail and in his other hand a pair of Dr Peppers. He sets the pop on the roof of the car. Opens the door and leans in a little. Hold this, will you?

The boy takes the pail and puts it between his legs. His father reaches for the pop and gets in and hands the boy a can.

Are we drinking it now?

Why not.

Thanks.

They peel the tabs and drop them in the ashtray. Then they drink.

Cold, says his father.

The boy nods and burps out his nose. How many did you get? he says. And he looks at the bucket.

His father says, Three.

Need that many?

How would I know?

The boy shrugs. And his stomach squelches.

Hungry?

A little.

As am I. Not far now.

His father starts the car and pulls back onto the highway, and the boy looks at the pail. Can hear them knocking against the sides. He puts the pail on the floor between his feet. Has half a can of Dr Pepper left. Doesn't drink any. His father flicks the blinker, and they turn down a gravel road. Then the gravel stops and there are only dirt and potholes. The birch trees gather like a crowd round a body. In the side mirror, the boy watches fallen leaves leap and wrestle then fall back to the road. They pass rutted laneways—a crow on a gatepost—that lead between big evergreens to cabins boarded up. Then a dip and a turn and there is the lake. The colour of blackboards. Here and there on the far side a few cottages, but not a boat on it.

Just us, Dad.

His father says nothing, but his face is calm. He slows down and pulls onto a widening of the shoulder where there's a green public wastebin and then a boatlaunch between dried-out cattails. He swings left a little—there's a small yellow cottage across the road—then backs the trailer down the slope. Around the corner of the cottage run two dogs—a small black Scotty and a big white sheepdog—and they stop at the laneway and bark.

Pay them no mind, son. They carry on like that.

The boy and his father get out, and as they're putting the boat in the water, a big man with a thick black beard comes out of the cottage and calls to the dogs. They stop barking and lope back to the cottage but look back a few times like they're saying, We're on to you. The boy's father waves, and the man waves back and lets his dogs in.

Know him? says the boy.

Not really. Spoken to him a couple of times. Decent bloke.

The man stands on the stoop as the boy and his father unpack the car. The boy takes the gaff and says, Where does this go?

Out, says his father, of harm's way.

Along the side?

That'll do. Frogs?

Oh, says the boy. Then gets the pail. Here okay?

That's fine. Right. Life jacket.

The boy bows his head and over it his father pushes the fat orange collar. Wraps the ties and knots them.

You wearing one?

No.

Water's kind of choppy.

I'll be all right. Now. The most important.

The boy looks in the boat and says, What.

And his father nods at the car. That tea and cooler, he says, I'm famished.

The boy says, I'll get them. Sees that the man has gone back inside. Gets the cooler and Thermos and says, Lock it, Dad?

If you like.

The boy locks the car and gets in the boat and sets down the Thermos and cooler. His father tells him to sit down— the boy does—and then leans and pushes.

Mind your hip, Dad.

I'm all right.

His father heaves and hops, and they're floating. The bow slowly turns counter-clockwise. His father takes an oar. Pushes off. Stands up. I'll just get by you, son.

The boy leans.

Ta, his father says and sits by the motor. Paddles a bit, and then he just looks. So does the boy. Straight ahead, about two hundred yards, a pair of smallish islands. Like the Group of Seven, but realer. And more sad.

His father primes the motor. Third pull it starts. He opens the throttle, but not so much, and the bow rises only a little. The boy leans on his knees and blows on his hands. Thinks of his mother, wax paper, and cake. The islands get bigger. His father veers toward the one on the right, and ahead, the boy sees weeds in the water like slow motion exotic dancers. His father cuts the motor. Trees lean over the islands' edges like drunks just waiting to sick on themselves. To the left are lily pads. They drift nearer, and the boat's bow turns a little. His father hefts an oar and turns the boat around completely. The boy looks over his shoulder. His father says, Best you cast away from the weeds. Into the deeper water.

The boy says, Okay.

But first, says his father, give us that Thermos.

Here.

Ta. Oh.

What.

Should have brought another cup.

Mum probably put one in.

His father opens the cooler. Indeed she did. Now, what's this?

The boy looks in the cooler—cake in Tupperware and the wrapped sandwiches—and his father says, She's written *S* on these ones. Salmon?

The boy taps his chest and says, No, me.

Eh?

They're for me. No butter.

Ah. Right. Well. Your sandwich, sir.

Loin and mushrooms.

Cold roast beef will have to do.

And cake.

At lunch. Give us your cup.

His father pours tea—Get that in you, lad—and they unwrap their sandwiches. The boy tests the tea against his lips. Sips and swallows. Heat in his throat and chest. Then they bite and chew.

She used, says the boy, the posh mustard, Dad.

His father nods and swallows. About halfway through their sandwiches—the beef's a little tough and tires out the jaw—he says, Let's get ourselves set, son. We can eat and fish. He puts down his sandwich and reaches for the tackle box and says, Give us your rod. The boy hands it to him, and his father says, Watch. Fixes a leader and ties on a Red Devil. This, he says, is a classic lure, son. Catch just about anything.

Muskie?

If your line holds. It's just ten pound.

What's yours.

Thirty.

That muskie at Ecky's—

Monster, I know. But most muskies round here are perhaps thirty pounds.

That's still big.

Not as big as you. Not nearly. Now, this reel isn't like your old one.

Open face.

Yes. More control of your cast—with practice. See my thumb?

Yes.

Holds the line. Then the motion like so—lift your thumb—it's away.

Do one.

All right.

The boy watches the lure wag in the air as the line and reel whirr. Then *plish*, the lure lands, and his father starts reeling. Neither too fast, he says, nor too slow. You don't want it to sink and then snag. Keep it moving and then—he flicks the rod this way and that—try that to give it a nice switching motion.

The boy nods. Watches the wake of the lure as it gets nearer the boat and skims the surface then lifts. His father reels in a little more then hands the rod to the boy and says, Try.

The boy releases the catch on the reel, and the lure drops.

His father says, Thumb first.

And the boy reels in. Holds the line. Releases the catch on the reel. His father leans back and points and says, *That* way.

The boy casts.

But the lure flies off to the right and plops in the water.

Less arm, son. More wrist.

Okay.

Reel in. You'll snag.

The boy reels in. Tries again.

Much better, son. Well bloody done.

Thanks.

The boy reels in and jigs—Like that? he says, and his father nods—and he imagines the tug and the sudden bending of the rod and the high-pitched zipping of the line, and he would land it—he swears he would.

You're all set, says his dad. And then starts to prep his own line. The boy looks back. Sees the hook his father chooses. Like a baby gaff. His father picks up the pail and pops the lid, and the boy looks away and casts again and starts to reel. And has to look back. His father reaches in the pail and then there is a frog in his fist. Puffy chin. Blackbead eyes. The dangling legs. His father holds the hook between his thumb and two fingers and then—Little bastard!—the frog squirts free and hops onto the seat beside the boy. Grab it, son!

And the boy does reach, but not very fast, and the frog hops over the side then *ploosh*, and the boy watches it kick out of sight. Looks at his father who says, Little bugger!

And the boy tries not to laugh.

Mind, says his father, your lure.

The boy reels in.

Jumped right out my hand, it did.

I saw it, Dad.

I said mind your lure.

The boy reels in and casts again and watches his father reach into the pail and say, *This* time.

The frog does nothing—no sound, no squirms—as the hook slides then pops through its chin and its mouth. The boy looks away. Looks back. His father lets out line then lobs the frog—*plash*—over the pads and plays it across and just under the surface. The boy looks at his half-eaten sandwich. Swallows tea. Casts again. Watches the dangling frog as his father finishes reeling.

How long will it last, Dad.

What.

The frog.

About as long as my patience. Tricky work, this.

His father lobs the frog a second time, and the boy casts again—his hands getting cold and his wrist kind of tired—and reels until he can see the lure. Then he just lets it lie. Wind picks up. The small boat drifts. Massive clouds pass over the sun, and the light on the lake changes like a big dimmer switch. The boy looks across the water to the car and beyond it to the cottage and its smoking chimney, and if they started the boat now, they could be on shore in no time—he knows this—but this place feels far from everywhere, like places in dreams that you know but do not know and that feeling that he and his father will always come back here and everything will be as it is just now. The slateblack water. The fishscale sky. But his father. His father is whistling softly—very softly—Glenn Miller music, and the boy watches him switch the rod to his left hand and reach inside his jacket and take out the silver flask with his initials on it. He unscrews the cap and takes a wee nip and then pours some in his Thermos cup. Swirls the spiked tea and has a big swallow then whistles some more, and the boy remembers his mother—bagging her old dresses. Slowly he jigs his rod and watches the lure rise into sight and sink again. Rise into sight. And sink again.

After a while, he sees weeds and looks around—they've drifted between the islands—and then at his father. Who doesn't seem to be fishing. Just sitting there. The boy lets him be. Looks toward the open water. He'll need a real long cast. Stands—his dad doesn't notice—then whips the rod behind him. It bends in the wrong direction, and his father screams.

The boy turns round. Drops his rod. Stares lockjawed at the lure—hanging like a leech from his father's left cheek.

Fucking hell, boy!

Oh God, I'm so sorry!

His father—eyes closed—sits very still and breathes through his nose. Barely opens his mouth and says, Son, sit.

The boy—hands shoved in his hair—breathing fast and shallow says, I'm—

And his father says, Sit. Now. Come here. Slowly.

The boy scooches toward his dad.

I need you to look.

Okay.

Did all three catch?

No, says the boy, just one, just one.

Is it through?

Through?

The skin.

No.

Settle. The tackle box. See it there?

Yes.

Open it.

Okay . . .

Pliers.

These?

The blue handles. Yes. Hand me those.

His father breathes out and cuts the line and then says, Now, pass me a hook.

Which one?

Any fucking one.

Dad, it's bleeding.

Pass me a *hook*. Right—now, watch.

His father puts the barb of the hook between the pliers and snaps it off. See?

The boy nods.

I need you to do that, his father says—and he holds out the pliers—but first you'll have to push it through.

I can drive.

What?

The boat. We can go to hospital.

We are—listen—an hour away from the hospital and I'm not driving there with a bloody fucking lure hanging from my face.

The boy wipes his nose with his wrist. Dad, I can't.

His father breathes out. Softly prods around the hook. Give us, he says, the pliers.

Sure?

He nods. Takes the pliers. Holds his breath and snaps off—grunting—the other two barbs. Takes out his flask. Closes his eye. Pours liquor over his cheek and the nose of the pliers and his fingertips. Then he drinks the last of it. Tosses the flask toward the front of the boat. Puts his thumb to the curve of the hook. Breathes in. Then leans to the right to sick over the side but it's half in the boat and the smell of it.

The boy clamps his teeth.

His father says, Son, you'll have to do it.

My hands, says the boy. And he looks at their shaking. His father holds the left one then places it against the top of his head and leans hard against it and says, Just pop it through.

Okay.

The boy pinches the base of the hook and—his father growls—pushes like he's threading a lace through an eyelet. The hook pops through. His father breathes out *hwah*. Grabs the pliers and leans his head toward his shoulder. Feels with his fingers and lays the pliers along his face and snips off the barb. It shoots away like a tiny silver wasp and then his father slides out the lure. Looks at it in his hand for a moment. Then tosses it in the water. Leans on his knees and breathes like a boxer who can't answer the bell.

The boy pushes the back of his wrist against each eye and blinks and looks at his father and then—it jitters—at his father's fishing rod. *Dad*, says the boy, and he points just as the rod starts rattling along the side of the boat.

Then the boy lunges. Grabs the rod's handle and gets to his knees, and the rod bends nearly double. But the boy holds on as the reel spins like a tire on ice. His father reaches round him and holds the rod as well and says, I've got it, son, I've got it! The boy lets go. Leans back with his father as he reels and pulls. Pulls and reels. Duck under, says his father. But the boy only watches as the big fish—like the lake spat it out—writhes in the air then splashes and thrashes then dives again as the boy's father says, Blood and fucking sand!

Then the line goes slack and curly.

And everything is quiet.

And the boy sits between his father's arms staring at the spot where the muskie was. And then his father's right hand lets go of the rod, and when the boy turns around his father is looking at the blood on his fingertips. And then he touches his cheek again and looks at his fingers as though they had lied. Then he wipes the blood on the leg of his pants and says to the boy, Go have a seat.

The boy moves up the boat and sits and watches his father reel in the slack line and look at the end of it. Wonder, he says, if it swallowed the lot.

The boy looks at the water and imagines the mangle of frog-and-hook in the muskie's mouth. Then he shrugs and says, We should go, Dad.

His father's eyes are glassy and wide. But he puts down the rod and turns to the motor.

And on the way into shore, he reaches for the pail and tosses the last frog over.

An old green pickup passes the launch and the boy's father waves it down. It turns into the laneway of the yellow cottage and stops and the man with the beard gets out. Meets them at the launch. The boy's father cuts the motor and the man says, How did it go? Then he notices. The boy looks down and his father says, Bit of a mishap. The man leans forward and grabs the bow's handle and pulls, and the boy steps out and helps him. Then his father steps out too. A little wobbly. The man looks at his face. Fish jump up and bite you?

The boy's father laughs, but not really, and the boy says, It was my fault.

The man says, Wanna come in? We got ointment.

The boy's father says, If there's a hospital nearby—

And the man says, You know Glanisburgh?

Heard of it, yes.

Go down number 7. Turn left on 30. Half hour tops.

That's what we'll do, then.

I'll watch your boat. You go on.

Very kind of you.

No bother.

The boy's father drives with one hand and holds Kleenex to his face with the other. The boy's mother keeps a box in the glove compartment. They use most of it, and in Glanisburgh see a church letting out. His father pulls over. The boy runs across the street and asks a lady in a hat like the Queen. Follows his father into Admissions then down to Emerg but they won't let him, so he sits in the waiting room beside the ambulance drivers' office. Hears the static and garble of the radio. Football on the telly. He glances at the tired- and sick- and sad-looking people and shuffles through old magazines about hot rods and jet airplanes. Looks up and sees his father in the doorway. Gauze and tape on his face. The boy follows him to the car, and the drive back to the boat feels like ages.

He put it back on the trailer, Dad.

Bloody good of him.

The boy's father gets out and walks toward the laneway, but here come the dogs. He stops. Waves. Gives a thumbs-up. The boy looks at the cottage and sees the man in the living room window waving back.

They quickly pack the car, and while his father hitches the trailer, the boy gets in. In the rear-view watches him turn for a moment and look toward the islands. Then—as they pull away—his father says, Some fish, that.

And the boy says, Massive.

Then they don't talk 'til 28.

Dad.

Yes.

Will it mend?

Son.

Yes.

Shush now.

The boy looks out the window and presses together his trembly lips.

In his room, he can hear their voices but not their words. Outside, the light is fading, and the moon is already out like a blind eyeball. He sits on his hands at the edge of the bed. Can smell the mince and 'nips. After a while, his mother knocks and comes in and sits beside him on the bed.

Sure you're not hungry?

The boy looks at the floor.

We're not cross.

The boy looks at her. Then down again.

It was, says his mum, an accident.

What if it was his eye.

It would still be an accident.

He'd be blind.

Well. Half.

It's not funny.

Suit yourself. Supper's there if you want it.

The boy lies down. Curls toward the wall. His stomach growls and he gives it a whack. Footfalls again—his father's this time. But they go past the boy's room. Down to the basement. The boy lies there a little longer and then gets up and walks softly to the kitchen. The dishes not done. His place still set and a glass of milk. He peeks into the living room. Sees his mother on the chesterfield. One finger tap-tapping the arm as she looks at the turned-off television like an old movie—the kind that makes her sad—with singing and dancing and dresses to die for.

THE DOOR OPENER

As he lifts the sag of leatherskinned rope and ducks underneath, the boy looks down. And does not look up as he walks to the blue. Turns and sits on the small, hard stool and breathes out his nose then smells his own sweat and the sweat of others still working out. Behind him, the lash and crack of hard, fast skipping. To his left, the smack and gasp of hit heavy bags. And in his mouth, the tire-like taste of the lime-green guard on which the boy bites down and—he cannot help it—gags. He works his jaw. Dislodges the guard. Sucks back spit. Swallows hard. Looks at Billy Sims, who is over in the red and probably the only sparring partner in the same age group—twelve to fifteen—the boy can easily beat.

But Billy's dad is here. Wearing just an undershirt—his arms all tattoo—even though it's March. Used to be a boxer. Now he's just a brawler. Real name's Terry. People call him Four Ball. That's how he did the guy who was living with Billy's mom. With a four ball. At the Legion. In a sock. Gets out on weekend leave now. And he's looking across the ring. Looking across the ring and listening to Dale Turner, one of his friends from the old pool hall, who's talking into his ear. Four Ball nods and laughs through the space in his teeth and keeps looking at the boy.

And the boy bows his head. Eyes the fraying laces on his left boot then watches the sleet—so fat and hard it's almost hail—smack and splotch and then slide down the old and dingy windows. And he feels behind him now the absence of his father. Hands in the pockets of his well-pressed trousers. Sucking on a mint or a Fisherman's Friend. And shouting out instructions—*That's* it, lad, interrogate!—that make other people laugh and jackdaw his accent. He pays them no attention. Used to be a boxer—a passable one, he said—in the British army. But now he teaches math and has a bad hip and is still installing—three days on—the Stanley automatic garage door opener that the boy's mother gave him for his forty-third birthday. It is hard to square the man who limps and mutters in the cold garage with the man inside the photo albums. The man in khaki. Or in the snow-white trunks and singlet. When the rose on his shoulder didn't look like a bruise. When his legs looked like Greek statues. It is hard to square. And the boy has told his mother he does not want to box. But when he thinks of his father, he does not want to quit. Shoves in his mouthguard. Clears his throat.

Over in the red, the club's old coach and owner, Mutley

Wells, is taping Billy's gloves and giving him the talk. Billy squints against the smoke and nods a lot, and when he jumps on the spot, his blubber jiggles. He's maybe five two. Weighs one fifty. Throws bazooka combos. But can barely see three feet. Sits in the front row at school and still has to squint. The boy tells himself to stay outside. Where he'll be nothing but a blur.

Mutley grabs hold of Billy's wrists and brings his gloves together and then turns and walks across the ring like it's the end of a very long road. The boy looks at the old humped back and at the wrecked face. The stubby Player's Special pinched between long wax-yellow teeth. Mutley is always smoking. Rattles when he breathes. But was middleweight champ of Scotland before the Korean War. In the pictures and clippings from his fights—they're on every wall—his busted face looks almost like the Elephant Man. And when he kneels and takes out his tape, the boy looks at the mangled ear and the veiny, bloated nose. You could probably fit a pencil lead in one of the wide black pores.

Once he's laced and taped the cuff of each glove, Mutley buckles up the boy's headgear and around the fag end says, Remember what ah telt you.

The boy nods once like boxers on the telly.

Use that jab ae yours.

He nods again.

But keep this one *up*, says Mutley, and he grabs hold of the boy's right wrist. Lifts the glove chin high. And the boy holds it there and nods. And Mutley says, *Throw* it as well, yeah?

The boy blinks. Thinks of times he could have—thrown the right *bang*—but didn't.

Mind me, says Mutley.

Around his mouthguard, the boy says, Sorry.

Combinations, says Mutley. Like ah've showed you. But don't stand still. You know what that wan's like—Mutley jerks his sausagey thumb at Billy Sims—in he'll come like a herd ae fuck'n elephants.

The boy nods and looks over at Billy, who is watching his dad show him vicious crosses. The thing with Billy is don't hit him too hard or too much or he flips. Caught Pete Marshall—a pretty good boxer—with a Hail Mary hook last month, and laid him flat out cold.

Mind *me*, says Mutley, who makes a V with his fingers and points it at his gunky eyes.

The boy gives his head a shake. Looks steady at his coach.

These aren't, says Mutley, bloody stilts you're on. He whaps the boy's left leg and his right leg, and the boy blinks and nods again. Use them, says Mutley, right? Stick and move. You've got tae stick and *move*.

The boy breathes deep—gags on his guard—and nods.

Right, says Mutley, and then he drags his right leg up and braces himself and slowly stands then looks over the boy's shoulder and shouts, Angus!

Aye!

We're waitin on ye!

Right!

Behind him, the boy hears Angus—Angus Wells, Mutley's youngest son—give the speed bag one last bash then run toward the ring. Angus is sixteen and always fuckin furious. Face like a fist with freckles and toilet-brush red hair and probably the best boxer for his weight and age group in all of Ontario. Biceps like halves of a five-pin bowling ball shoved beneath his skin. Mutley makes him ref the junior sparring. It's the only time Angus ever laughs. But he helps his old dad down out of the ring. Then takes off his bag gloves and scoots beneath the ropes. Rolls and stands and points at each corner.

The boy stands—his galloping heart—and behind him Mutley removes the little stool.

In the middle of the ring, the boy stands as tall as he can and reminds himself to stay outside and be a blur. He looks at Angus. Then at his boots. Then at Billy—his spidery mustache and the taut purple pimples on his shoulders and chin.

Angus says, Right. And he pinches a nostril. Blows out the other. And says, I don't want to see any *shite*, hear me?

The boy nods. Billy nods.

Good clean fightin an' all.

The boys nod together.

Right, touch gloves.

They touch gloves, and Angus pushes them farther apart and takes a step back. Flicks his hand and then says *Box* like it rhymes with hoax.

The boy gets up on his toes. Billy squints. Comes plodding on.

Sims, says Mutley, chin!

Billy tucks his chin.

And Angus looks at his father. Points at the boy and says, Look at the dancin on this one. Then he laughs.

And Mutley says, Mind the fight or ah'll brain you.

Angus screws up his face and looks disgustedly at the space between the boys. Ah said *box*.

The boy moves in.

Billy knows—because Mutley's told him—about the boy's

jab. Keeps his gloves up. But his arms are so short that his belly may as well have a target painted on it. The boy glances at Mutley whose face says, What in fuck are you waitin on?

And then, beyond Mutley, the boy sees his father, standing tall but round in the shoulders and watching the fight like theorems.

Then he looks back and—*boof*—Billy tags him. Right in the nose. Four Ball yells, Yeah! The boy's eyes water. And Billy starts swinging like the boy is a cloud of blackflies. Move! says Mutley. And his father says, Lateral, protect! The boy covers up and ducks and dances to the left. *Pick* your punches, Billy, says Four Ball Sims. Be patient, now, be patient!

But Billy's breathing hard.

The boy blinks and sets himself. Three hard jabs into Billy's gloves and Billy keeps them up so the boy sticks one into Billy's belly and when his gloves come down he jabs him hard in the face. Mutley says, Combos! And the boy's father says, Muck in, lad, muck in! Over Billy's shoulder, the boy sees Dale and Four Ball sneering. He brings up Billy's guard again and—does not know where it comes from—lands a right hook on Billy's jiggly belly. Billy makes a sound like a cat hacking hairballs. Doesn't counter. But the boy backs off, and Mutley says *Ach* and Billy just keeps coming on his stumpy legs and taking jabs and getting redder and redder. His eyes water and Four Ball says, *Slip* his jab and hook him! Slip his jab and *hook* him! But the boy dances and stays outside until Angus stares daggers and says, Try a little boxin.

The boy moves in and jabs and jabs, and Billy tries to counter but he doesn't have the reach then the boy lands a right on Billy's nose. Backs off. Sees the blood. Morris, says Matley, the kid's found his right! But the boy's father just looks on and says nothing. Billy sniffs hard. Swings wild. The boy says, Easy. But Billy barrels in. The boy jabs. Billy's head rebounds. Four Ball yells, Slip it! But the face on Billy. The boy knows it. Has felt it on himself when he was sparring tougher guys. You feel paralyzed. Babyish. Like you were born just to stand there and take it. The boy jabs softer. Connects and says, Sorry. And scowls at Angus when he laughs. Billy starts squealing like a garbage bag of kittens. And in he comes with the Hail Mary bombers.

Move! says Mutley.

And the boy does move. Right into Angus. Stumbles. Rights himself but—*bang*—catches one on the ear. The world goes like the space between two channels. He steps back—is on the ropes—and as though from a distance his dad says, Protect. He covers up as best he can and hopes for Time. But Angus doesn't call Time. And Billy keeps squealing and bashing and Four Ball cheers and says, Dig his fuckin heart out! Between his gloves the boy sees Mutley point at Four Ball and shout. And then he takes a right in the ribs. Feels his whole frame shudder. Drops to one knee. Billy keeps bashing. Angus darts in. And the boy drives a right—*boof*—into the cup of Billy's groin protector.

Billy folds and falls and flops around bawling like a devastated walrus, and his dad comes charging round the ring. Points at the boy as though he's an assassin on a balcony and yells, Low fuckin blow! Low fuckin blow! Angus kneels by Billy, and then looks at the boy. See you, he says, *out*.

The boy stands and cradles his side, though it doesn't hurt so much, and eases himself between the ropes. Four Ball Sims is a few feet away and glaring at him around Mutley, who has a hold of his shoulders. The boy's father walks around the opposite corner and light gleams in the strands of spit as the boy lets his mouthguard drop into his gloves. He is about to say he didn't mean to. It just happened. But his father nods toward the locker room and just says, Change.

The boy jumps down and walks past guys who have been watching, and all of them stare as though he stole money from their jeans. At the door leading to the hallway and locker room, the boy looks back. Sees Angus and Mutley kneeling either side of Billy, who is sitting up now, and they are rubbing his back and patting his shoulders and saying things to make him laugh. Four Ball has one hand on the edge of the ring as he looks between the ropes at Billy. Then he looks at the boy's father, who is over by the windows. Hands in pockets. Head down.

In the locker room, the boy drops his mouthguard in the garbage bin. Tears at the tape on his gloves with his teeth and then at the laces. Shakes off the gloves and unwraps his hands then drops the wraps in the trash as well. Unbuckles his headgear. Punts it.

Pete Marshall sticks his head in and says, Why'd you *do* that?

The boy sits on a bench and says nothing.

Four Ball, says Pete, is pretty pissed off.

The boy looks at Pete and says, Shut your mouth.

But when Pete goes, he stands at the sink and looks in the mirror at the twitching of his jaw. Grinds his molars. Peels off his singlet and tries to tear it in two but can't. Just bends over the sink and sloshes water through his hair. Hears Billy's dad yelling in the hallway. Then Mutley. Then—softer and calmer—the voice of his father. The three of them pass by the locker room. The boy opens the door a bit and leans out and looks down the hall. In front of the trophy case, Mutley is standing between the two men. Look pal, I'll no tell you again. G'wan outside and cool off, or I'll ban you.

Ban me? What about fuckin—

Watch the language. Ah've telt ye. We'll sort it.

As Mutley talks, the boy watches his father—his taut face and the little bobbings of his Adam's apple—then Angus sees him and crooks his finger and points at the floor by his feet.

Eyes down, the boy walks into the foyer.

Right, says Mutley, you'll be speakin with Billy in a moment, but you can start with Mr. Sims. Then Mutley looks at Billy's dad and says, Ah'll see how wee William's doon. Then he leaves.

Above them, the fluorescent lights hum. The boy looks at his father. His father nods once.

Sorry, Mr. Sims.

Look at the man, says his father, not the floor.

The boy looks briefly at Terry Sims's face—his gargoyle face—and at his hideous arms. And says, Sorry. Sorry I hit Billy. Then, under his breath, as Sims snorts and starts to walk away, the boy says, Bastard.

His father says, *What.*

And Four Ball stops. Turns. Makes a fist. And cocks it.

And the boy says, Dad! Hears the awful bone-to-bone crack. And sees his father's head rebound. His forelock lift. And his arms spread wide as he falls—falls hard—to the wet, filthy floor.

Everything thrumming like amperage in wire, and the boy looks at his father lift his head and shake it. And then he looks at Four Ball. Looks at Four Ball and backs up a step. But puts up his fists. His shaking fists. And Four Ball laughs. And then the boy's father is up, and Four Ball says, Want it again? But his father walks by as if he doesn't hear. As if Four Ball isn't even there. He walks and he stares straight ahead like a clock-work man, and as he reaches for the door says, Son, come.

The boy, bare-chested, thinks for a moment about his bag and his coat and his clothes, but he runs past Sims and out the doors where sleet hits him like a spitting mob. Fists either side of his chin, arms in an X across his chest, the boy leaps puddles in the parking lot. His father opens the tail-gate. Leans in. Takes out the plaid blanket. Drapes it round the boy and says, Get in.

And the boy sees blood—like fine red thread strung along his father's bottom gum and in between his teeth. He opens the car door and gets in and starts to shiver.

His father starts the car and cranks up the heat. Then he says, Belt.

The boy buckles up, and his father turns on the wipers and the lights and then he backs out.

Looking for Sims, the boy sees only Angus and Mutley. At the club's front door. Holding the boy's jacket and his gym bag and watching the car drive by as though it's a hearse.

A pickup truck passes, and the driver leans on his horn and gives the finger, but the boy's father doesn't blink or flinch or speed up at all. Just stares straight ahead and drives like he does when they visit strange cities in Quebec. When the boy's mother sighs behind maps. At the corner of the highway and County Road 7, the light goes red, and the boy yells out. His father brakes hard. They slide to a stop. The boy breathes out. Looks at his father. Sees that his chin is discoloured and trembling.

Dad.

Be quiet.

The boy holds his breath. Stares at the curling letters on the fake wood glovebox—Cutlass Supreme—for the rest of the way. At the end of their drive—the big evergreens in heavy grey light—the boy's father reaches for the remote that is clipped to the visor. The garage door lifts. Then shudders and goes down.

His father stops the car and again tries the button.

The door does the same.

His father unclips the remote from the visor. Gets out of the car. Hurls the remote right over the trees. Tries to lift the door—it only budges—then holds his hip. Limps back to the car. Reaches in and turns it off and takes his keys. Slams the door.

The boy gets out and steps in a puddle and grinds his teeth and runs through the sleet. Leaps up the stoop. Watches his father poke the key at the lock. Reaches for his wrist and says, Let me. His father whacks his hand. Drops the keys and kneels for them. But stays there.

In the front hall, the light goes on. Footfalls—his mother—in her knee-high boots. She opens the door and smells of Chanel and Aqua Net and looks very angry—they must be late for dinner or Bridge—then sees the boy in the blanket and gasps.

What's happened?

The boy tries to answer but when he looks at his dad—at the hunched and shuddering back—it's like a mouthguard turned the wrong way was shoved past his teeth and he's choking.

MID-FLIGHT

The boy in 11A could easily be Slav, but his Gogol is in English.

Pardon me.

Yes.

You are Russian?

No.

United States.

Canada.

Do you know Kingston?

Where I went to grad school.

Queen's University.

Yes. That's right.

Last week I lectured there, in the department of Russian Studies. It was very nice, I say, when in fact I found the students dull, and the city even duller, but kindness pays when travelling. The young man in any case seems unimpressed. You are in Korea why? I ask.

He says, I live there.

Teaching?

ESL. Yonsei University.

This is remarkable. I was there yesterday.

Lecturing?

The last. Two months of travel. Tokyo. Bologna. Now, home.

For a moment, his mouth relaxes, and I sense in him a need to talk, but he only nods then sets upon his Gogol. Maybe I unnerve him. God knows I unnerve myself. This dewlapped stranger when I shave, staring dully back at me: the bloated nose and yellowing teeth; thin white hair and man-tits; slathering my lower back with analgesic ointment, and the rest of me with spray-on scent, masking leaks and seepage. In younger days I slept on flights. Now my guts begrudge me a rubbery slab of chicken, and I watch without sound the ending of a film about alien invasion. Flushed Korean men, meanwhile, bark for beer and soju, and whiny brats are doted on by their harried mothers. Mine bore thirteen of us and could arm wrestle farmhands. Now, she drools and soils herself, and after my long absence, will struggle (I am told) to remember who I am through an opiated daze.

Miss?

Yes.

Vodka.

Ice?

No. Moment.

I turn toward the boy.

Drink for you?

No.

The attendant bustles up the aisle. She and her coworkers look as though they were produced in test tubes and petri plates. A laboratory beauty, perfect and undesirable. With a bow, she serves my drink. I sip it and (never able to read on planes) watch the TV screen, which now displays statistics: Altitude and Speed and Time to Destination, an appalling figure counting down by intravenous minutes. My lumbar aches. My arsehole itches. I swallow an anti-inflam, and the stats give way to an ad for the next World Cup, which Japan and Korea will cohost. Beneath a football emblazoned with world flags, a caption says:

Dream for All
2002

Programming then resumes: hidden cameras capturing the surprise and indignation of shopping mall customers pinched on the backside by actors posed as mannequins, and camera-laden tourists squirted by fountain cherubs. The boy watches briefly, and unvoiced laughter shakes his frame, but soon he goes back to his book. Reading like an infantryman on a long, wet march. Leaning slightly toward him now, I try (the light is dim) to read my mother tongue translated into his.

However many directors and higher officials of
all sorts came and went, he was always seen in the

same place, in the same position, at the very same
duty, precisely the same copying clerk . . .

Do you know, I interrupt him, that Dostoevsky said: All Russian literature descends from Gogol's *Overcoat*?

Yes, he says, I've heard that. Then continues reading.

. . . in it, in that copying, he found a varied and
agreeable world of his own . . .

What takes you to Russia?

Using his thumb, he holds his place, and says, I have a friend there. He used to live in Seoul. Got a job in Moscow. If it had been Berlin, he shrugs, then I'd be going there.

And your book would be Goethe?

Probably, yes.

Movement, then. Not place.

Anyplace. Except for Seoul.

You don't like it?

I do not.

Why do you stay?

Money.

Canada—

Canada. I drove a cab in Canada.

Economy is so bad?

I knew PhDs on minimum wage. Landscaping, data clerks. Thousands of us over here, teaching pidgin English.

I try to interject, but the words now tumble out of him.

The first year I worked at a dinky private institute. Hagwons, they call them. Taught kids this high. Teacher, game! Teacher, game! Hanging off my pants leg. Thought a university would be different, dignified. So I came back. Salary. Free time. But what is there to do? The few Korean profs I know are overweening, idle. And the expats, lost. You meet the odd diamond. But the rest feel like redundancies. Plastic bags blown about by global economic winds. I see them at bars and pubs, entertaining newbies with the same recycled stories. Give me half the nights I've spent in kitschy neon dance clubs, drinking toxic beer. Sixty-dollar cab rides. Ten-dollar coffees. Bridges and whole apartment buildings—a shopping mall—collapse, and Koreans keep on blathering this Asian Tiger crap. Pointing at you. Laughing. A man at a urinal once tried to *piss* on me—sorry, I've . . .

It's all right.

Way too far.

I understand.

He holds up his little book as though it were redemption, and he starts to read again. I would like to slap the back of his head. Wake *up*, spoiled fool. At the same time, I am fond of him. Stay with me, in my flat. There are many books. We can read aloud. In your language and mine. The nights are very, very long, and there is much to learn.

Where, he says, surprising me, do you live in Russia? Moscow?

Yes, but I'm going to Petersburg now. Where my mother lives.

That's nice, he says.

No. I'm afraid she has cancer.

The world falls between us like a severed head.

He says, I am sorry.

She is very old. Will you pardon me?

Of course.

Long minutes pass in the cramped toilet. I smell of mouldy goat cheese, and the lighted mirror vivifies my bogeyman visage. Young man, I was as fair as you. As fair as you, and tall. Mama, do you remember? I am Nikolai, your third.

ANIMAL CRUELTY

Slow down, she said.

    Fuck we goin, anyway.

    She said, Warsaw Caves?

    I said, No.

    Well. You make a suggestion.

    Why are we always doin this? Every fuckin weekend.

    She crossed her arms and pouted, and I mimicked her.

    Don't, she said.

    How you look.

    Don't.

    Silent, sweaty miles passed. I threw savage looks at her pale fat calves and recessed chin. The old man had this phrase,

Steak not macaroni. There was something to it. When I first met Larissa, back in winter of third year, I could run my fingertips up and down my ribs. Now I had a gut. Mushroom caps, cheese sticks, potato skins, fajitas. She loved eating out, and she always paid. In return, I played the role of boyfriend, confusing utter pointlessness with existential depth.

Cat World, said the sign, *10 KM*.

I braked and hit the blinker.

Larissa said, Sure?

What else is there, minigolf?

We drove a straight stretch of road, farmland either side. Then right on a concession.

I said, There was this book. Glanisburgh Public Library. Think it was just *Big Cats*. I signed it out all the time.

How old were you?

Eight or nine. Read it back to front, over and over and over. Memorized their markings, how far they could leap. Favourite prey. Habitats. Used to trace the pictures, then practise freehand. It was the only year I got a Good in Art.

We parked in the all but empty lot. Aside from high fencing, the place looked like a hobby farm.

What do you think, Larissa said.

I shrugged. We're here.

August had nearly ended, but it was thirty-odd degrees, a wet, heavy heat.

The clerk said, Adults?

Students, said Larissa.

We showed our cards and went through the gate. In big

180

chain-link enclosures on our left and right, long-tailed monkeys swung with ease toward us. Their gaze black and beady. We followed a gravel path. Gibbons, lemurs, peacocks, but most of the cats had withdrawn into shade. On the far side of a grassy field, two lions lazed, gold-brown lumps. An ocelot shimmered past the dark mouth of its den. Up ahead, a mother and her boy had paused and were staring. *Puma concolor.*

Mumma, did it die?

No, he's just sleeping.

Wake up, stupid cougar!

Tyler, let him be.

Wake up wake up wake up!

The animal cracked an eye. Larissa veered and pointed.

What, I said.

Leopard.

Head low, it loped toward a corner of its cage, sharply turned, and climbed a crooked tree limb. Its saggy belly flapped. Its coat was dull and matted. Now it jumped down and made the same dizzy loop. Again and again and again. Flies meanwhile buzzed around a bloody shank of meat. The cage stank of piss-and-straw.

Larissa said, I'm leaving.

Wait, I said, and followed her.

She broke into a run.

ACKNOWLEDGEMENTS

Special thanks from a proud misFit to Michael Holmes and everyone at ECW.

For critical help in critical times, thanks to Jon and Susan Davis.

Earlier versions of some stories appeared in *Prairie Fire* ("Lure" and "Petty Theft"), *The New Quarterly* ("MacInney's Strong"), *Best Canadian Stories* ("The Door Opener" and "Stragglers"), *Queen's Quarterly* ("Mid-Flight"), and the Galley Beggar Press Singles Series ("Dogshit Blues"). Thank you to the editors of these publications.

Thanks to Tom Leonard for allowing me to quote his poem, "Good Style."

The Tools by Phil Stutz and Barry Michels helped me to become a better ambassador of myself.

Thanks as well to Ryan Simpson, Jason Heroux, Stu and Susan LeBaron, Barb and Orm Mitchell, and Gary and Pauline O'Dwyer.

In memory of David Glassco, my teacher and my friend.